Manhattan

Underground

by

Baker Crawfield

I dedicate this novel to my family and friends

~Baker Crawfield

we are for each other: then
laugh, leaning back in my arms
for life's not a paragraph

~e.e. cummings

Chapter 1

If I close my eyes I can still smell it. That smell of motor oil when it hits the hot outside of an engine. The smoke from it filling the car. When I came around the corner I saw the kids, a girl and a boy holding hands, crossing the street. I swerved, pulled the wheel hard away from them and that's the last thing that I did. I could hear them scream. That hellish choir. The front end of the car collapsed. I didn't see anything. Just a smear after the kids. An airbag, hard canvass against my face. First slammed forward, then pushed back. My head. I felt something touch my eye and it stung.

A stream of nightmares: I was being pulled out of my broken body. Voices whispering my sins. Everything stained black and red. A tunnel of strobelights. People saying my name. An angel appeared with a long spear and jabbed me with it – over – and – over – again. Blood flowing out of me. Shadows came and lifted me over their shoulders and tossed me into the deep dark waters ~ I sank. Deep. Deeper into a darkening abyss.

When I thought I was finally drowning and waiting for the terror to be over, I started to hear music. Strange and familiar. I fell to the floor of the abyss and a cavern opened beneath me. It sucked me farther down. All the while the music growing louder.

Chapter 2

I woke up in Columbia Presbyterian
Hospital, a few blocks from the accident. I don't
remember the ambulance. I don't remember the
flashing lights, the sirens. I don't remember the
car door opening or being lifted out and onto a
stretcher. On a hospital bed. I was scared. I wasn't
sure what was dream; what was real? I started to
cry. I don't know why. I couldn't sort out my
thoughts. My vision was bleary. I hurt.

It was night. The room was dark. The
vitals monitor pulsed and glowed. A white spray
came in florescent through the door window.
Beep. Beep. Beep beep. The tempo of the monitor
started to rise. The volume started to escalate. My
skull started to shrink. The walls were closing in.
My head was caving in. Pressure.

The door flung open. The room flickered
and flashed into light. Then I saw the white coats
come in. I slipped back into the water of my
dreams. When I emerged, I noticed a woman
knitting in a chair not far from my bed. I looked at

her. I watched her carefully move strings of yarn over and under and through. Over and under and through. Our eyes met and she startled. She held her chest. The long needles still in hand. She placed them aside and came to me. She told me I was alright.

I didn't feel all right. I felt lost. I felt alone. And I was in serious physical pain. Knowing I was in a hospital, I couldn't be certain where I was. I'd hit my head pretty hard. I smashed in my forehead and my cheek. I couldn't lay my head on a pillow without pain swimming around in my head. I noticed my own slow blinking. Even with the pain medication they gave me, there was no comfortable position for my head. That comforting nurse let me know that I was lucky to be alive. It's easy to die from bleeding from the head, she said and I smiled at the lack of subtlety of her accent, the meaning behind her words was all I heard.

Then came a flash – stepping into Grandma Trudy's SUV. I winced and in that shutter moment, a recoil. The crash. The unknown fate of those two kids haunted the darker recesses of my imagination. Their parents looking down on me like the Gods their children saw them as – each with one eye filled with remorse, the other blazed with hate. All my body went limp. My head flopped back against my shoulders. I couldn't breathe. My lungs filled and emptied but it meant nothing at all. And then a sudden jolt of blinding pain. A blackness came over me in a white flash. George, George. I could hear her and that is all. She touched my shoulders but her voice was fading and I couldn't feel her touch anymore. Even the pain seemed to slip away from me as I sunk.

Chapter 3

Released from the darkness again, released into the hospital, that thin mattress, the astringent smell, the dull whining glow of fluorescents. A different woman was standing over me. She was rigid and serious. Her white coat rubbed against my arm. She pulled up my eyelids and shined a little light in there. What day is it, she asked. I answered. What's your middle name, she asked. I answered. Do you know where you are, she asked. I answered. She turned to the nurse. She said, get him ready for the test.

Think about being a bullet inside the chamber of a gun. Tight walls circulate around. Then a powerful metallic thunder. Demerol was my coping mechanism. They gave it to me for the physical pain of my injuries. It was a fuzzy, disconcerting feeling of secured helplessness. I was laid up in that tube for an hour with light blazing all around. At the end of the test I was limp and ready for bed. They took me back to my room. I laid down. The nurse told me to rest. I had to take that test two more times. I couldn't stand the thought of it. Back into the darkness. Into my cold, wet inner world. Shivering through icy waters, I sailed down to barracuda level and stayed there until sunlight through the hospital room window shined in my eyes.

The end of that day brought an end to my MRIs. Once again I was limp like a boxer at the end of a hard fight. I couldn't tell if I'd won or if I'd lost, but I had the bruises to prove I'd been fighting.

Another day passed and my test results came back. No concussion, no terrible brain damage, just some bruising. I was thinking pretty hard during my time in the hospital. It was a major setback. All I was looking for was a modest apartment and a job. Tough town; and this is just the beginning. My nurse came to talk with me between lapses of unconsciousness, sleep and tests. It turns out that her's was a Filipino accent. She was born and raised in Manila, but lived in Tenafly, New Jersey, a pleasant little suburb not far from Grandma Trudy.

Mrs. Nims, my nurse, my caretaker, my friend. She told me about her daughter, a struggling actress in Los Angeles; her husband the

ex-navy seal; her empty Manhattan apartment.
The apartment was originally meant for her
daughter. She was supposed to study acting at
NYU but ran away to California with a Lebanese
boy named Bernard. So the one bedroom in
Washington Heights was empty and it was me
whom she asked to fill the space at really a
reasonable price. I accepted the room and the ride
back to Grandma Trudy's house.

On the ride back to New Jersey, just before
we got on the GWB, she looked at me dead in the
eyes. She asked me if I wanted to know the fate of
those two children. Are they dead, I asked. Mrs.
Nims started to chuckle – her chuckle turned into a
belly laugh. Her laugh turned into tears. No, she
said. Mrs. Nims reported two children in good
health, minus a terrific scare. What street you
Gramma live, she asked me. I pointed Mrs. Nims
in the right direction and she dropped me in front
of the door. I thanked her for the ride. She said
that Mr. Nims would be by in a couple days to
help me move-in to the apartment.

When I knocked on her door, Grandma,
Gram was beside herself when she pulled me in
the door and hugged me. I hugged her back.
Little woman. She made tea and we ate lamb. We

11

talked for a few hours. She told me about when I was a baby. About my parents when they were young. About herself when my father was my age. And then it was late and she sent me to bed. I slept in late. Not unnoticed by Gram but she allowed it considering my condition.

A few days later, Mr. Nims was at the door, his polished Cadillac parked behind him. Are you ready, son, he asked. Yes, I answered.

Chapter 4

Mr. Nims, with great suspicion and hesitance first sat next to me quietly in his modern classic and then watched smoking as I took my boxes up to his daughter's vacant apartment, one box at a time. He looked at me with great regret, as if I was an unwanted suitor breaking into his daughter's life without his consent and beyond his power. But I was just renting a little one bedroom in a part of Manhattan that is easily qualified as *sketchy*.

When the last box was on the floor of the otherwise empty apartment, he shook my hand and looked in my eyes. He looked defeated. As if this was his final concession, an admittance of his defeat by his daughter, or a final realization that she had chosen to leave. I shook his hand and told him that I would take good care of his apartment and I meant it.

It was a lonely evening for me in an empty room with the stuff that I'd kept from all of the years leading up to this moment. I started calling my friends and I talked to one and then another and another until I finally fell asleep on the floor.

Chapter 5

The buildings abounded the streets and the avenues breathed and sweated with dappled people. Among them I felt an awkward welcome that was my new feeling of home. I found a bodega around the bend, a little Latin corner store. It was like a 7-Eleven, but with Goya and prickly pears, a sprinkling of Doritos and potato chips, soda, beer, bread, milk. I bought enough food for breakfast, a dozen eggs, some butter, bread, a carton of orange juice. I took a mango for a little experiment and when I bit into it I couldn't believe it had taken me so long to feel the grainy, velvety texture, to taste the tangy, sweet juice. I love mango!

I looked over my new kingdom, about 150 square feet of freedom. No parents, authority figures of any kind. Just me. Me and the scattered mess of things that I'd amassed over the years. I started opening boxes, suitcases. I found my towel and soap, toothbrush and paste. I decided to go ahead and start my day.

When I was clean and ready for a new day, I frowned looking at the mess of my possessions. I sat on the floor and looked at all of it. My mind started spinning, searching for alternate ideas – anything I could do to put it off, to procrastinate. But there was nothing. I stared off into space for a few minutes. I went to the kitchen and poured myself a glass of water. I sat near the pile of my stuff and started opening and dumping. After all my possessions were splayed out on the living room floor, it hit me. I needed a bed. Distraction at last! I put on my hat and locked the door on my way out.

I found a little mom-and-pop mattress store around the corner. I bought a cheap full-size mattress and box spring. I carried them home one at a time – first the mattress and then the box spring. I tossed them on the floor of my bedroom and cooked some more eggs for lunch. Then back on the floor. Books, clothes. I'd already unpacked the dishes, pot and pan. I folded my clothes and put them in a corner of the bedroom. So much to buy. I knew I'd be broke in a month.

For all my internal bitching and moaning about unwanted chores, it took no time at all to sort out my stuff. The last thing I unpacked was my laptop. The tool of my trade. This is my trade. Words on pages. It's what I studied. My chosen profession. The thing is—it's really a ridiculous choice. Especially for a middling student in a nothing special college. But all that is behind me and I am unrealistically optimistic about this one part of my life. I am willing to sacrifice every other facet of life for success in writing. I am too naïve to live. I have no fears. Maybe I should. But I am certain it will all come to a joyful conclusion. And it makes me smile.

I went back to the bodega and bought a six pack of beer. I ordered a pizza. I sat on the floor with my back against the wall. I looked at the piles of paperbacks in the corner of the living room. I turned on my computer. I hijacked a wireless signal and downloaded a movie. I ate and drank and watched. Tomorrow, I thought. Tomorrow I would do something. Until then, nothing; I'm a lazy slacker.

Chapter 6

I had to take a test before The Stand would hire me. The bookstore. I'd taken this kind of test before. Tough if you don't know shit. But a breeze if you're a fan of fiction. There were two columns on the flip side of the application. One had authors, the other had titles. I had to match the correct author with their correct title. It made me smile. Test? It was like having to color in a picture to get a job at a poster shop! I was tempted to write quotes near the titles: Hemingway's The Sun Also Rises, *I misjudged you…You're not a moron. You're only a case of arrested development.* There was also Beloved by Toni Morrison, *A man ain't nothing but a man. But a son? Well, now, that's somebody.*

Bookstores. I like those movies about the people who work at bookstores. They wear comfortable sweaters, often host beards, glasses. They are often cynical wits and ardent observers of social activities. Arguments about Nietzsche's passive involvement in the evolution of the Third Reich. Or, who was Shakespeare's best clown,

Festy or Bottom. The people I met at The Stand
were misanthropes often educated and one or two
hyper-educated in subjects like Medieval
Literature, Philosophy, Sociology. They were
introverts and drab and sad. And this job was not
going to pay my rent. I needed something else.

After work I'd go to Union Square, about a
quarter block away from the store. You've seen it
in movies, the statue of Washington on his horse,
the crescent stairs, the performers, the crowds,
Virgin Records across the street, Whole Foods,
Filene's Basement, Shoe Mania. I liked sitting on
the steps. Not much for spending-money, save my
savings, I opted for people watching. That crazy
guy – big goofy sunglasses, a spaceship hat, loose
colorful clothes. I think he was on drugs. He'd
walk around talking to strangers. I envied his
uninhibited nature. But he was, you know, crazy.
Though I must admit that the highlight of my
television replacement was the women. Strong.
Intelligent. Assertive. High heels. Strong curvy
legs. Style and sex appeal. I had no idea what I
was getting myself into.

My mom calls it blowing off steam. My
dad calls it exercise. I call it a long walk home. I
lived one hundred and fifty-six blocks from where

I worked. It's not so terrible. There's a lot to see in all those blocks. Besides, I could have taken the subway. I opted to walk through one of the most rapidly changing and evolving cities in the world. I lived in Washington Heights. That's North-West of Union Square. The island itself is a compass. The East River, Brooklyn and Queens are in the East – the Hudson River and New Jersey are in the West – Harlem and the Bronx are North – the Statue of Liberty and Wall Street are South. The streets run East and West. The avenues run North and South. I started on Broadway, which at that part of town is anorexic. It's the western edge of Gramercy. It's a short walk from there to Flatiron where there's that big triangular building that looks like an iron. That's where Eliot Spitzer's prostitute lives, or so I've heard.

Broadway splits off in two: Broadway snaking up to the West, and Columbus Avenue veering off to the East, but still certainly on the West Side. I didn't know the city very well at the time, but I remembered seeing Broadway in my neighborhood and relied on it to get me home. Besides, I had a healthy curiosity, mostly due to the movies and books. But you're not really walking the streets of New York film history until you've tucked yourself into the folded pages of Wall Street which was in the opposite direction that I was walking.

34th street was, to my surprise, quite drab. A bunch of very suspect shops selling trinkets and jewelry, knock off perfume. I didn't see the miracle in it. It was dirty, dark, and it gave me the creeps.

The city cracks open at 42th street and the dark night turns into a showcase display. Broadway spreads out to earn its name. The billboards sing and dance in the walled city skies. The crowds swell and the lights replace the sun.

Ten blocks up and it starts to fade. The buildings darken and the streets quiet to a calmer pace. The channel of Broadway swoops open at Columbus Circle on the South-Western edge of Central Park. It's where the Columbus fountain is, and Trump's hotel overlooking the park and the globe that leads to the subway and that new mall, and the Mandarin Hotel. Tourists and pigeons like to hang out here with bicycle taxis, street vendors, panhandling musicians, carriaged horses. It's a good spot to pop a squat and let the legs rest.

I followed Broadway through the Upper West Side. Passed Julliard. Passed Figueroa's.

Passed Barnes and Noble and Banana Republic, Lincoln Square and the best –hands down – movie theater in New York City~the Lincoln Center Theater. Two stories of glorious architecture with adorning elephants. If you hit it up, go up to the balcony seats for no extra charge. Into the West Eighties, cafés like Ouest and staggering pre-war buildings with beautifully furnished rooms and degrees on the walls and some dirty secrets in well-shod closets. A few small bookstores, and clothing stores like Barnie's CoOp. I walked down Edgar Allen Poe Street and back. Then up through the Nineties and into Morningside Heights where Columbia and Barnard students live and hang out in clean, well-lit places. I walked through Harlem. Colorfully painted buildings and a part of the street itself was painted brightly. Eventually I made my way up to 170th street. I walked by Columbia Presbyterian Hospital and shuddered in remembrance.

Chapter 7

It's hard to walk around in a place famous
for its wealth and work at a bookstore for a hair
above minimum wage. It's not like in the movies
or TV when a guy who works at video store and a
girl who works in a coffee shop finish off their day
and sigh in an apartment the size of one story of a
suburban house. That simply isn't reality. Reality
is that my entire apartment is the size of the
bedroom that I grew up in. I grew up in a modest
household in the Pittsburgh area. In Pittsburgh I'd
have gotten a lot more bang for my buck, but it
would still be Pittsburgh. New York City. It's
stylish and sexy. It's vast and fast and impossibly
complicated. Its possibilities are mythical.

These are the things I was thinking while I
was stocking shelves at The Stand. Daydreaming
like anybody else with a job as meaningless as
mine. But these are the thoughts that spurred me
to act. When I got home that night, I sat and
worked on my resume. There are no Greek words
attached to my degree, but my grades were

respectable and I worked hard. My experience in my field started at my involvement in my high school newspaper and stopped with the college newspaper. Other than that, it's a video store and my first job, washing dishes at a local sports club. They let me play pool for free. It was a selling point at fifteen.

I spent the next month spewing resumes to any and every magazine, newspaper and publishing house that I could find. I expected a call back from one or two of them. But every time I looked at my phone, all I saw was the time. I knew that I wasn't hot-shit, but I had a hard time believing that absolutely no one wanted me, no one even considered me. Damned to a bookstore? Stocking shelves…forced financially out of New York and back home a failure who couldn't make it a few months. Laughing stock of my college friends. And I thought it was going to be so much easier. Welcome to New York. Welcome to the real world. That's what mom told me when I called her to complain. Hang in there, that's Grandma. Dad. He stayed quiet about it. We talked about sports. He was watching his beloved Yankees finish up the series. Autumn was setting in.

September snugged into the city with a
northern breeze. I hit the streets with another
round of resumes. Less hopeful. Stubborn.
Pigheaded. Ambitious. Foolish. Foolhardy.
Absurd. Arrogant. Optimistic. Youth personified.
I remember walking into that broad and
overwhelming lobby. It was nearly Christmas and
my birthday had passed with lonely remembrance
of joyful gatherings in my past. My palms sweated
and my hands gripped the tissues in my pockets.
My dad's suggestion. The elevator door opened
with a ding that triggered a fear I cannot explain. I
hit the button. I rose up a few levels. The
receptionist scanned me. Take a seat, she said.
Audrey will see you soon.

She took my hand and smiled. I sat across
from her in a small chair. She sat behind an
enormous ornate desk and looked at her computer
more than she looked at me. She asked. I
answered. She looked at me coyly and I
questioned if it was smugly. She said she'd let me
know, stood up and walked to the door. We
touched hands again and smiled again and I was
back in the elevator again. Descending. Back into
the broad lobby and out onto the streets. A cab. A
bald man. A woman. A street vendor. A group of

high school kids. I started to feel sick. I walked to the park and sat and breathed. I didn't let the thought form. I didn't ask the question. I watched the people walk by without judgment or curiosity. I didn't look at my phone. I felt it was all over.

Chapter 8

Three weeks later the phone rang. It was a new year. I was the same person. Stuck. In the same spot I've always been. Stuck in almost. Stuck in not quite. Stuck in too bad. But the phone rang. And I answered it. Hello. The news I'd been hoping for. The news I'd been praying for. Holy shit! You can start Monday. Nine a.m. sharp.

I wanted to celebrate but I had no one to celebrate with. I wanted to go out. But I didn't know where to go. I refused to sit at home smugly enjoying the thought of my entry level position at a prestigious news magazine, Newspeak. So I acted like what it was I wanted to be: respected, talented – a little more money wouldn't hurt. I showered. I shaved. I even trimmed my nose hairs. I put on my best clothes, clothes that couldn't dare compete with New York City fashion, but I wore them anyway.

I stood uncomfortably in the subway station waiting for a train. I hadn't yet gotten used to the grim sight of the tunnels, the occasional rat, the smell. At 168 street, the tunnels are deep underground and the air is thick and stale. But the train came dragging hope with it and I stood inside of it rocking erratically on my way downtown.

Of course I walked into the wrong bar. Milk Bar. Not far from Union Square, my safety zone. It was a lame version of the milk bar in A Clockwork Orange. But they had a great selection of beer. I had a tall glass of something or other. I drank slowly and thought wonderful things to myself. I felt like I was on the right road. The road I was meant to walk. On my way up to becoming what I'd always wanted. I mused and sipped until I finished my beer, unaware of the others, casting off their weekday lives. I was shedding my skin, shedding the bookstore and welcoming a new beginning. Sure, I took a job in the mailroom instead of the job I asked for, but still…

It was the wrong bar because I was dressed for a small town church and I was in a place that didn't resemble anything close. When three girls approached me I thought it was a good thing. My luck had seemed to change for the better and I was enjoying the upswing. But reality is a terrible thing. Girls don't approach nothing special guys in nothing special bars for what I hoped they wanted. Instead I got grinning, chiding, cruel women. Smile. Finding a cruel woman in a town like this, throw a stone. I'm lucky they didn't ask me outside and kick my ass. I took the ribbing with a cockeyed grin and left with as much pride and self respect as I could hold onto. This was not the bar for me. All the same I wasn't ready to go home.

I went barhopping one beer at a time until my pockets were empty. Mostly I was pushed aside in each. Sipping, standing in corners and watching others, familiar with each other, laughing and having good times. I was jealous of them. I wanted to be one of them: good clothes, nice taste, interesting conversations about politics, style, music.

Midnight trains don't run often in Manhattan. I was under Eighth Avenue hoping for the A train but willing to take the local C. I wished I had a book with me, or at least my MP3 player, but no. Nothing to occupy my time. I took a dirty seat on the bottom of the steps. Across the tracks a man stumbled with his case. He dropped it listlessly and flicked it open. He pulled out the

29

old brass, a stained sax. He slapped the pieces together out of seeming old habit. He blew – a quick blow through the scales. It took him no time. He took a step back into the wall. I think he was drunk. Suddenly. Composure. A smooth, cool note that he slid into a sweet melody. But it was the C train that arrived. Out of luck. A long ride home.

Chapter 9

I woke up on the floor. Light peeking through a window. Orange juice in my hair. A glass flat on its back near my outstretched hand. I slipped in the juice on my way up. I reached for the glass and landed on my face. Shit. I laid there for a moment taking in the pain. Nothing serious. I made it to the kitchen and dropped the glass in the sink. I mopped the living room floor and finally a shower.

I ordered some Kung Pao chicken and pork-fried rice and read through Atwood's *Surfacing*. A beautiful feminist work that actually made me feel guilty about being a man. But I enjoyed it all the same, the reality check, the reminder of the sex wars and the total complication of love and life. She took me far from New York City into Canada's French Quarter. It was peaceful to sit and read. I felt invited by her into the minds of intelligent women. A demand to be separately equal to men, and possibly more powerful, but as a man myself, I found that aspect

to be egoistic. She left me with a strange unease.
A perfect feeling for the day.

   I went for a walk and watched the sun set
on the Hudson and I smiled at New Jersey. It was
then I decided not to lay this weekend to waste.
Maybe the city would be kinder to me this night.
Maybe not. I'd let the night decide. I dressed
more casually and expected nothing. My hopes to
be some kind of exotic artist may have been a bit
foolhardy. On my way downtown I started
thinking that maybe during my stay in NYC I was
more likely to inhabit the role of the fool. A good
Shakespearean sideshow who managed to center
himself in a story. Some Festian character. But
more likely than that, I'm meant to be Bottom.
Posing as king of the forest while actually being an
ass. Hoping that Goodfellow might toss me some
dopey, beautiful queen.

   I found myself walking down St. Marks. I
only know the history back to the punk rock era:
Iggy, Patty Smith, Blonde, The Velvet
Underground, Warhol, The Sex Pistols, The
Ramones, etcetera and so on. The punk influence
existed still in fashion and music, but very few
wore it with the same attitude and addiction. The
leather and metal clad crowd in youth thinned as I

walked east. Quiet seeped into the street. The
architecture took precedence here. Townhouses
turned apartment buildings could only be
described as quaintly European with a New York
flair.

A small crowd. A large sound. Seeping out
into the street from a small café. It was
intoxicating. The rhythm. The melody. The genre
closest to my heart. A love that I cannot explain.
Jazz. Jules, if it weren't for the music, I probably
wouldn't have even noticed it, but I did. I noticed
it and I stopped and I looked. I hated going out by
myself. Just not as much as I hated sitting at home
alone on a Saturday night. I was nervous to walk
inside. Where would I sit, or stand? Who would I
talk to, if anyone? I couldn't take a repeat of the
night before.

I pulled myself together and descended the
three steps that led to a sitting area before the
door. People were sitting and smoking and talking
theatre and politics and music. They all looked so
interesting and unusual. I walked inside. If it
were the twenties, it would have been smoky and
mysterious. But the new laws dictate a new scene
and the air was fresh and clear, deleting any sense
of mystification that may otherwise have been. I

took one of the few empty seats at the wraparound bar before anyone dared seat me.

A man with a crisp haircut and a lax way about him asked me if I'd like a drink. I asked him to recommend a beer. He smiled and pulled a bottle of Duvel from under the bar. You like, he suggested to me after pouring my glass most of the way full and left me the bottle. The beer was nice, but a little stronger than what I was used to. I looked around the dimly lit bar. It may not have been cancerously smokey, but it did have a certain something. It had a character all its own. An attitude. The people were wonderful to look at. They smiled at each other and ate and talked. They were comfortable and relaxed, away from their daily routine, escaping into the possibilities of a weekend. I wondered who lived in Manhattan and who were from out of town. I wondered who was American and who was foreign. It was so interesting to me, the thought of a city so filled with foreigners. I don't know exactly what my fascination was. But it was.

As I looked around, I wondered if there were someone there for me to talk to. I imagined not. I've never been the type to approach strangers. Though I did see someone who made me want to break my streak of solitude. She sat at the end of the bar drinking from a glass through a straw. It wasn't lust that I felt toward her. It wasn't love or passion. It was simple curiosity. She had something. A confidence. An attitude. The delicate line of her shoulders was proud. The line of her neck, more bashful. Her face was intelligent. I started walking toward her. I felt comfortable because I wasn't going to attempt to pick her up. I wasn't going to use a line. I wasn't trying to convince her to go to bed with me. I just wanted to find out who she was because she seemed to be so much more than me. But as I was making my way toward her, she moved away from her own solitude and into the arms of a welcoming group of musicians. And suddenly, I envied her. There was no longer a guise to my emotions. The veil fell. I envied her easy assuredness. But most of all, I wanted myself to be part of a group of interesting people. Tonight was the night to pursue that simple ambition.

I lost my seat. I stood there and watched them. They talked and laughed and drank. They had cases of instruments. The drummer was setting up his kit. I wanted to walk up to them, but... That's just not me. It would take all my confidence and bravado to approach one stranger. She kissed the saxophone player, a tall, lean, bald guy. I was jealous of him suddenly. I couldn't explain it to myself. I had no feelings for the woman. What made me jealous was what they symbolized. They were love. They were style. They were music. They were complete. They were part of something. I was a worm on a string. Unsure of my fate. Wriggling in fear of what might be and what might not be. Alone.

The musicians brandished their instruments. The drummer with a soul-patch and black and white, silver tipped shoes. The bassist with his stand up bass, just waiting for the chance to spin it around and pluck out a rhythm. A three man band fit the space at Jules. The saxophonist left the girl in the sage dress and took the stage, center. He pushed out a long, smooth note. The drummer danced his sticks softly on the high-hat. The bassist came in last, after the tempo had risen, and burst with blump, heavy notes.

I liked the sounds that they made. It was a high tempo, a hot beat. Three men on stage losing their minds! The man with the sax blowing his face purple. The bass man following his strings in circles, jumping his shoulders and clucking his head. And that crazy drummer was all over the place. He must've had four good beats going! Melodic pandemonium. It put a smile on my face and I wasn't the only one. The mystery girl was smiling too and swinging her hips and it seemed to me that if I was going to investigate the lives of these strangers, that was the time. I put my empty glass aside and made my way to her. Her back was to me. She was facing the band, staring at her love, that sax man and I felt embarrassed to interrupt, but I was compelled. I tapped her shoulder. She must have been so far away in some other world with him because I startled her and I didn't mean to. She turned to look at me. The tips of my fingers still touching her shoulder. She looked at me almost incredulously. I wished I'd thought of something to say, but I hadn't, so I just said hello, my name is George. I removed my hand from her shoulder and held it out for her. She looked questioningly in my eyes and then at my hand. I and my hand were criminals to her at that moment. Since she said nothing, I said, I love this music. They have a great swing. Her head tilted and she smiled a toothy smile and I relaxed a bit. I told her I saw her with the sax man and had no intentions of seducing her. She leaned in to hear that gem and responded with tension-releasing laughter, true laughter, childhood laughter. It made me smile. She then asked me the only question she could think of – so what do you want then, George? I knew what I wanted but I didn't know how to say it, not without sounding like a dope. I smiled and looked at her eyes. She was waiting for an answer. I said, you all just look so interesting. I wanted to see if it was true. She smiled at me again. She put her hand on my shoulder. She told me to stay and that we would talk later and she turned away from me. I asked her, her name but she didn't look back. She stepped up onto the stage and smiled at the audience and then she looked over at me specifically. She lifted the mic to her lips and said, my name is Alice. I was touched and at that moment I decided that I certainly would stay to see what would unfold as this evening wore on.

The sax man soothsaid a steady, modest C note. Bass man thumped out a soothing rhythm and the drummer made a little dance between his toms. Alice smiled shyly, gazed toward a small patch of open floor in front of her, took a breath and started to sing. Her voice was soft yet it captured every ear in the bustling room and soon that bustling simmered to silence to hear her sing. The sax man slid up to B-flat. He swayed the sax at his hips and tipped it slow and rhythmically from side to side spilling the sound all around. Alice's voice grew stronger. The drums and bass pulled up louder behind her. A few breathes passed my lips before I realized what was being sung. My ears forgot to register. I didn't understand the words. She was singing in French. It was French and it was Jazz. I wondered, Edith Piaf?

Alice stepped off the stage and walked toward me smiling. She asked if I liked the song, but didn't wait for an answer before beaconing the bartender. He poured her a glass of water and she stole a straw from the bar. She returned her gaze to me, waiting for an answer to her original question. Are you French, I asked her. Now she wore a full-cheek smile. Did you like my singing, she asked. Yes, you made the room stand still, I said. She took a drink from the bartender and handed it to me. Thank you, George. Cheers. Cheers, Alice. I took a sip. It tasted like pure alcohol. What it is, I asked. Vodka Martini. You are French? Yes, of course. Of Course. She turned to the band. They were playing some hot, fast, maddening rhythm. I looked at them sweating, blowing, banging, thumping, spinning, raising, lowering, smiling. I sipped. I looked at Alice. She swayed her shoulders to the bass, her hips to the sax, and her foot tapped to the drums.

We stood and watched the band. Nothing more was said between us for some time, and then she went back on stage. I sipped my overwhelming drink. They played. She sang. They all went together so nicely. I think it must have taken a lot of practice. Maybe that's one thing I could learn from all really good musicians: relationships take a lot of practice. The band as a whole fit and understood each other. Drums and bass worked together to back the lead instrument who toned down to slip behind the singer. Not to say there was no innate competition for the spotlight! They each pulled solos. Different songs at different times. When that player's rotation came up, they played like it was a competition. Bass player thumping out a double beat, the sax blaring, drums gone wild. And then they'd come together in a fervor. Until, of course, the singer stepped on stage. At those times they were all fine and mellow.

I sipped my drink until it started to warm in my hand. The room shuffled and dealt. Then the music stopped. Everybody clapped. The musicians exited the stage and following Alice – they walked toward me. I expected the sax man to be eyeing me suspiciously, eagerly awaiting my explanation for chatting up his girl. But that was not the face he showed. Alice introduced me and sax man, named Sam, who smiled and shook my hand and asked me what I thought. I didn't lie. I smiled back. They introduced me to Joe, the drummer and Charles, the bassist. We took up a table in a corner of the room and another band went on stage. Martinis for all. Alice drank for the first time that night. It felt good to sit among them and I did feel welcome. The most bizarre thing…they were interested in me. Did I play? Where was I from? Siblings? What brought me out tonight? Cheers and jokes and laughter. Joe was from Williamsburg, Brooklyn. Charles, Kansas City. Sam grew up in Harlem. Alice was from a small town East of Toulouse, France. Sam and Alice met at Jules five years before I walked in the door. Sam and Joe had met in high school. Charles came to New York by rail with his grandfather when he was eleven. He met Sam and

Joe a decade later in Washington Square Park. The four of them had been together for years. Jules was one of their favorite places to play.

We stayed and talked until Jules was closing down. The staff was gentle when they ushered us out with a few other tables of late stayers. We exchanged numbers and made promises. I flopped into a cab and felt good, if not a little drunk.

Chapter 10

Sunday afternoon woke me with a smile. I was comfortable to stay at home. I didn't shave. I didn't shower. I played some music and laid in bed and read. I ordered Tex-Mex from a Chinese food restaurant. Watched a movie on the computer. Behaved like a total slacker without regret or remorse. In the evening I set an alarm on my phone and mused what my first day at a real job would be like.

Chapter 11

A little overzealous, maybe, I showed up at eight-thirty. I thought a moment on how to procrastinate, but I just walked in the building. I waited for Audrey for almost an hour. She seemed pleased that I was there waiting for her. She also seemed to be pleased with herself for making me wait. I've never minded indulging my employers' power-trips. They are the reason I'm making money.

We took the elevator to the third floor. I was happy it wasn't sub-level as I'd imagined. In fact, it was an open room with floor to ceiling windows. No cubicles. Two enclosed offices for the managers. I felt good about my fortune. I wasn't getting paid any great amount of money, but it was enough to eat, pay rent and bills, and even to go out on the town about once a week so long as I'm not trying to live the Manhattan highlife. I'd have to save up for a month or two for a night comparable to that. But I figured I'd have to at least once.

Audrey introduced me to Harold, the mailroom manager. Harold took over my introduction and Audrey kindly wished me well as she made her way back up the elevator shaft. Harold introduced me to the other manager, Isabel. Next and finally, Marc. He was a year older than me. He'd been in the mailroom for a year. He worked in a specialized part of the mailroom. His workload had increased and they hired me on to lighten his load.

Marc was a little less optimistic about his present and his future than I was. He was moody and jaded. But he was smart and occasionally pulled out an interesting insight into the city, politics, music, current events. He liked reminding me that he graduated from NYU with a journalism degree. He seemed to feel superior to me when I told him that I graduated from Penn State with a bachelors in English. He then made a vague comment about me being there in the negative. I didn't have a journalism degree; I'd never lived in a city; I was not hip or cool by any Manhattan measure. I had terrible dress sense, no real cultural exposure. Ok, he made it apparent that he felt superior to me. I shrugged it off. I didn't care much what he thought about me. I was happy to be working for a prestigious magazine. And I was happy with the appearance that I was going to get by in what the natives of New York City like to call the greatest city in world.

Chapter 12

Letters piled up quickly. I could see why Marc was so frayed and why he needed help. I'd say, after about a month, that we averaged about fifty letters a day, each of us. It seemed more like busy work than anything else. I read through letter after letter looking for letters to go to the editor. Sure, they were all addressed to the editor, but Claireborne didn't have time to go sorting through all this. Neither did the assistant editor or either of their assistants. They decided to filter the letters closer to the source. It was Marc's and my job to sort through all of them and come up with twelve, six each, letters a month worthy of print. It felt pretty prestigious a first job for me. Marc disagreed.

The daily monotony was engrossing in a coloring book kind of way. People are generally smart and interesting, especially when contacting editors and especially in New York. It was never easy making my choices and only one or two of the letters I found worthy would pass the editor's judgment.

Day in and out reading people's thoughts on current events left me in awe of how much all of this politicking effects the individual. Especially during times of war. I won't go into the details. We can all imagine the tolls on our neighbors' lives. Losing loved ones, jobs, faith. Watching their dreams slipping away from them. War, who knows what it was all really about, security? revenge? spreading democracy?

Many will stand firmly with their convictions whatever they may be and fight for them ceaselessly. I don't know, never knew what to think of it. I was just a kid with big dreams right out of school. The military has no use for people of my skill set. I never wanted to kill enough to actually do it. I didn't feel the war was worthy of my personal attention either. I didn't believe in it. I disagreed with it. It made me sad to read some of these letters. Right there in front of me the grief and anger of so many individuals. I thought about getting angry myself. But then I would have to act and I was far more interested in exploration. I guess I thought of myself as an explorer of sorts, just on the smaller scale of the world. I wanted to discover some of the magic of this particular city because of all the music and movies, books and paintings... There is magic in this city. Real Merlin kind of stuff and that's what I wanted to find.

Chapter 13

Another weekend snuck up on me. Friday night passed with no more than a lonesome evening including Chinese delivery and a few movies. All the reading during my weekdays shied me away from reading much on my days off. Though I did get into the habit of picking up a NY Metro on the way to work in the mornings. To keep up on local events. Bloomberg had been wooing the Olympic committee to choose New York by threatening to build a new sports arena.

Saturday afternoon was laundry and shopping and catching up with my household chores. As the sun set I couldn't help but think about Jules and the night that I met Sam and Alice and Joe and Charles. I hadn't been back to Jules since that night. Come to think of it, I hadn't gone out since I'd started this job. I had focused my weekends on nesting. I got a couch for the living room, a desk and chair for my computer. A shelf for my books. Still no frame to my mattress, but all good things eventually come.

I was sitting down, staring at a blank white screen, brainstorming my first New York City short story. I had envisioned so much during my preparations to come to this town. I thought about Cheever and Parker and the waves of influence on the art scene. My bizarre fascination with Jazz and Jazz musicians. They made the early carvings on the block that would eventually become rock and roll. They were brash and violent, tossed to the mercy of their own emotions and ambitions. Most importantly they were original, the original reckless musicians. Before them it was all symphony and structure. Jazz took away the structure around musical emotion, broke the basic barriers of tradition in the way the West understood it en masse.

My phone rang. I expected it to be Mom. She called at least once a month to see if I was alright. I just don't understand what it is to be a parent. I've never understood. But it was no one protective that called me. It was Sam. I was surprised and couldn't recall giving him my phone number. He said they were talking and I came up and they wanted to know if I wanted to hear them play again. I couldn't explain the empty feeling I'd had sitting at that desk. Grasping my ambitions

but feeling only my fears. Thoughts of my parents
and my little sister, family in general. Other than a
few scattered moments in college, they were all I
knew of the world. I'd sat to write about New
York City knowing nothing.

Chapter 14

They were playing in Tribeca. A restaurant he said was famous, called Trattoria. I'd never heard of it. But that doesn't mean anything. I had no idea what was going on around me. The city was so tremendous that the task of scratching beneath the surface was overwhelming. I mean, the buildings themselves seem endless; they hang over you and around you – they create the broad and narrow streets and paint the backdrop of every scene. The traffic, both automotive and human dictates the often fast-pace and erratic rhythm that sets the tones.

I hadn't been down to Tribeca before Sam invited me to hear them play. I liked the architecture in this part of town, the squat buildings felt old and reminded me of layered cake. Sam said they'd set up around nine. He said he'd meet me at the bar. He said there'd be more people for me to meet. He said we'd have fun.

It was dark when I arrived. The streetlights and lights from shops and restaurants twinkled on the concrete where puddles had gathered during the afternoon rain. It was jacket weather. Well in to March. Spring started to overcome winter; buds ornamented the branches on the small trees that lined the street. The streets were packed. People dressed like they lived here. All the wildly expensive designers you see advertised in magazines worldwide. They're all a bunch of models. That's what it was like. Just truly strange. I must have stuck out like a sore thumb. Nah, it takes a lot more than me to stick out in this town. I guess that I was just part of a background, but what an expansive backdrop I was a part of.

It was fun. Traveling from one end of the city to another. You see so much. Even underground. The crowds change in the subway as you rail from neighborhood to neighborhood. They are all very distinct and culturally independent areas that, all sewn up, create this whole city.

I started in my neighborhood, Washington Heights. It's mostly Puerto Rican, but safely Latin American. Very boisterous people who love to party and live life. The A train takes me south into

Columbia's campus and filter in some of the most prestigious college students in the country. I always tried listening in on some brilliant conversations, but what I usually heard were what you realistically might expect. They talked about their families and social events and dude, you got so wasted last night...college kids!

Then Harlem. Honest to goodness Harlem. Ok. I didn't know what to think the first time the train stopped at 125th street. The doors opened. No rap stars, no famous basketball players. I was kind of disappointed. But I didn't see all that many famous people when I first got to New York. Maybe a handful or two throughout the years. But I did get a chance to meet some of the locally famous.

Down through touristy Time Square. The tourists stuck out because they looked like they were at Disneyland with their I heart NYC t-shirts and stuff. Don't get me wrong, I was definitely doing my own tourist thing. I was just taking the long way around. I would love to come here some day and stay at the Ritz or Trump Towers and go shopping on 5th Avenue and in Soho and see shows on Broadway and have dinner on top of the Empire State Building. Maybe all in good time for me. But I couldn't do it in a week. God bless 'em, those tourists.

I got out at West 4th street. The NYU part of town. I like the trees in Washington Square. I like the fountain and the performers. There was a real Shakespearian feel to that park. I walked down through Little Italy and over to Tribeca. Mott street. I love the cobble stones. The smell of Italian food. It makes me hungry every time I walk through there. I'd usually stop at a pizza place and have a slice.

It was a little passed nine when I walked into Trattoria. I breezed past the hosts with a smile and took a seat at the bar. I ordered a Duvel and scanned the room for my friends. Through an amassing crowd, Sam appeared smiling. Alice at one side and his sax on the other. He drops his instrument near my feet and we shake hands. Alice and I kiss each others' cheeks. Society, huh. They order some drinks. Charles comes in panting, saying it's cold out there and he ran from the cab. It had started to rain. Joe showed up. His fullbrim hat was limp, wet.

We end up sitting at a table in the very back of the restaurant. I think it used to be a firehouse. Something about the pipes everywhere and the large open space with rough textures. A large rectangular bar centered the room. The tables, large and small, were set up café style. It was a pretty uptown crowd. Luckily I was put on the musicians' tab.

Kidd Calloway played the trumpet. He joined us in the back. It was a lively scene. The glasses were some purple, some green, one pink, some clear. And people kept pulling up chairs. We were talking Jazz and laughing. The musicians traded and rethreaded stories and adventures. And just as our group was about to become the loudest in the place, composure fell over our table. It was a strange blanket of calm that draped us. The musicians at the table pulled themselves together and stood. Joe, Charles, Kidd, Sam, Richey, straightened themselves up and headed toward the stage on the other side of the room. I sat with Alice at the bar facing the band. She was excited and smiling. The guys stood in front of three west-facing windows. Outside the windows, the streets were floating passersby through the city night. The sun well set. Joe twists his goatee. Charles plucks out a rhythm. Joe brings in a beat. They play back and forth and show the way they can play off of each other. Kidd breaks up the reverie with a call from his brass. Sam pushes out a flurry of notes. Richey slides in with his trombone. This was a big band compared to that night at Jules. Charles and Joe played off of each other song after song. Drums pacing while the bass set the parameters of rhythm. Kidd and Sam fighting for center stage with Sam slightly in the lead. Richey, the link between forestage and rhythm.

Alice appeared on stage. The fast and wild songs set aside. Joe brushed the symbols. Charles brewed a full bodied rhythm. The trumpet muffled. The sax slowed. Trombone…careful. She leaned toward the microphone like she was going to kiss it. And before she tipped it, she started to sing. In a crowd that wouldn't have noticed if a busser dropped a thousand dollars worth of dishes on the floor, they all startled to silence and turned to her.

We ended the night much as it began, at a large table in the back of the room. The witching hour came and left. The drinks were poured – the glasses, emptied. The conversations circulated like the *Sunday Times*. Arguments and jokes until the revelry broke apart, out of the restaurant and onto the sidewalks – into the streets. A couple cabs were hailed. A few walked in different directions. I found the A train heading uptown without much of a wait.

Chapter 15

Just before 9am, Monday. I scanned my
hand at Newspeak. High tech clock in. I sat and
started opening the mail. Physical mail. Email. A
few minutes later, Marc joined me. His cup of
coffee, the steam making its way over to me. It
smelled good. Marc waited a few minutes before
he returned my greeting. I hate Mondays, he said;
it reminds you of the week to follow. Are there
people who like their jobs? ... Do you think there
are, George? I looked at him. I'm content with
this job...for now, anyway, I said. He looked at me
suspiciously and confused. You, he said, you like
this job, sorting through these meaningless
afterthoughts? Look man, my contentment with
this job is about me being happy with myself. I
wanted to come to live in New York City. I saved
up and here I am. I needed to find a cheap
apartment and a job that would pay for it. I made
that happen too. Yeah, right now, I'm pretty
pleased with everything. It could all be so much
worse. My first job here was at the Stand, so, this

is definitely a step up. Besides, if you hate it here so much, why don't you find a different job? You obviously think you're qualified for a better job, I said. He looked at me. He looked a little different. He looked surprised and then his face changed again and he looked impressed. My bad, he said. I left him with the last word and we both went back to work.

The week wore on and I noticed that Marc had become more open with me. He also started to be nicer to me, which was nice because I had to spend 40-50 hours a week with him. I hadn't previously made the conscious realization that his miserable mood had started to adversely affect my own. But I did notice that his improving mood was helping my days' fluidity.

Work started to become more enjoyable all around and that feeling of drudgery each weekday morning had subsided into a meager curiosity of how each day might play out. And I started to make acquaintances at work. Work buddies, if you will. We'd even go to a bar around the corner on Thursdays to blow off steam. We'd all have something to talk about on Friday, our hang-overs. Some also got together on Fridays, but I'm more comfortable keeping some reasonable distance between work and social life. Besides, I didn't want to mess with the good thing that was starting between me and the musicians. I'd started hanging out with them pretty regularly. They dragged me all over Manhattan. They did shows in Midtown, Broadway, Soho, Tribeca, the Lower East Side, Wall Street even. It was getting to be pretty exuberating. I was starting to feel like somebody special, going to fancy restaurants and clubs, drinking for free, hanging out with large groups of interesting, well dressed people.

Marc offered up a new scene. New to me anyway. The remnants of the New York Punk scene is what Marc offered up one Friday afternoon at work. The ghosts of Iggy Pop and the Sex Pistols lurking in the alleyways of liner notes. The Ramones, the New York Dolls, The Velvet Underground and that whole weird speed-freak scene with Andy Warhol. Sure, these days it was the Strokes and Le Tigre and the Yeah Yeah Yeahs. But we were going to see some small, emerging artists which is kind of the whole idea of going to clubs like CBGBs and the Knitting Factory, a truck load of these hole-in-the-wall places peppered the crowded streets. This was much more an offer of a gritty subculture. I expected mohawks and piercings, tattoos and blood, torn clothes, cheap liquor, beer, drugs, street thugs.

CBGBs was going under the gun by the time I moved to the city. The bums had moved in upstairs and the lines leading into the venue thinned from all the panhandling. It was the end of an era with Hilly Crystal owing tons of money in back rent and taxes. I read about it in the Village Noise. But Marc was not talking about CBGBs, which he'd referred to several times during this conversation as a joke. Joke or not, it was an historic venue that I did want to visit before it finally shut down. I would end up seeing the last show ever performed in CBGBs, Dick Dale, courtesy of Noah Morgan.

It was Friday and Marc starts going on about his girlfriend, Zelda, who'd actually never come up in conversation before. I didn't even know he had a girlfriend. It was a subject that neither one of us had ventured into before, which seems strange to me. Aren't these introductory conversations that two coworkers might stumble upon in the first month of working together? All of a sudden it was Zelda, Zelda, Zelda! He liked saying her name. There was no doubt about it. It calls to mind Scott Fitzgerald's wife. She was a serious author in her own right. And it's one of the best videogames of all time. Apparently Zelda was bold and blonde and beautiful. She was the part of Marc's life that showed progress. He might not have a job that he values above all else. But he does have a woman. And admittedly, that is something.

By the end of that day, Marc had convinced me to join he and Zelda at the Mercury Lounge on Houston and A in the L.E.S. I like the Lower East Side, and so I rightly should. It's a little grungy but it's got roots that grew a transient, rebellious generation that appealed to the people my age in my particular mark in time. It was a slice of NYC that was reserved for aging kids.

I met them in line outside the Mercury. The doublewide street of Houston separated our side of the street from the other like the broad river that separates Manhattan from Brooklyn. It was a concrete reminder that we inhabited an island. A fact that I found easily lost. The first thing I noticed about Zelda were her thick blonde locks. Marc was beside her, hanging on to her. It was more than enamoration. It was inebriation. They had apparently started early. He bellowed out my name when I stepped up to them. I smiled and

told him I'd have to catch up. Zelda shook my
hand. She was nice and seemingly patient with
Marc dripping off of her. I was a little
uncomfortable. Marc was in no state to mediate a
conversation and Zelda and I didn't know each
other at all. We did our best to chat each other up
while we were in line. She told me about the band
that we'd come to see. They were called Apollo
Sunshine. I like the name; it reminds me of Sun
Ra. Marc started going on about Apollo Sunshine
and how the night was going to rock.

     Mercury Lounge was a tightly packed
place. A small venue separated into two parts by a
pair of French doors. The initial part was the bar.
The size of a doublewide trailer with forty people
blocking and trying to get to the bar. I ordered
three beers. I really didn't think Marc needed
anymore, but I didn't want to just grab one for
myself and drink alone and I also didn't want to
get one for Zelda and me and leave Marc out of the
loop. So I figured - worse thing would be it would
get warm in his hand. When I gave Zelda the
plastic cup-o-beer, she passed me her flask of JD. I
started to relax and hadn't realized how wound up
I'd been.

We maneuvered our way through the bar crowd, through the threshold of the French doors and into the more expansive showroom. We found a bare spot of wall and propped Marc up there. Zelda capped her flask and lit a joint. I can see what happened to Marc, I said jokingly. She laughed. I took a heavy drag of the joint and Zelda started to tell me how she and Marc had met.

He was a student at NYU. She was studying chemistry at Columbia. She was still in school when I met her that night. I tried to get her to tell me a little about what she'd learned about chemistry, a subject that I find fascinating, but she refused to get into that headache, as she called it. I smiled. She met Marc on her way to a party her freshman year. She got off the 1 train at 86th and Broadway. It was a house party.

There was Marc. Standing in the tunnel with his guitar case at his feet. Some change and a few crumpled bills inside. His guitar in hand. She said he was playing Nirvana's Polly. Their eyes had met. Marc had only been here a year and Zelda had just arrived. They didn't speak until she emerged from the subway. He caught up with her at the corner and started walking with her on the way to her party. She didn't remember what they talked about and she confessed the subject matter didn't matter. It was all tones of voice, their hands brushing lightly as they walked closely together. He walked her to the door of the building of the party. She didn't invite him to accompany her. She did give him her phone number. A week later they went to brunch and talked for hours after they'd finished eating. They kept the mimosas coming. Back then Marc had his eye on working for Rolling Stone as a day job while he and his band-to-be slowly made their own way to center stage.

Zelda laughed when she said that she was split between working on pharmaceutical and street drugs. Her voice broke when she confessed that either would be better than being a pharmacist. I just don't want to spend my life behind a counter filling scrips while other people get to do all the fun stuff, she said. She admitted that she hadn't created the next wave of party drug yet, but the possibility wasn't entirely out of the question. Just think of the money, she said. Just think of the jail time, I said.

Mic check. One two, one two. It's good, he said. Then a twang from the guitar. They were just about ready to start. Is that Apollo Sunshine, I asked. It wasn't. Sunshine was the headliner. These guys were the Bleeding Hearts. My beer was finished. Zelda offered me her flask. I sipped but it was too strong without a chaser. I said I'd be back and asked if they wanted another beer. The mainroom wasn't yet packed and getting back to the barroom wasn't too difficult. In fact, there were just enough people around to feel cool walking between them.

I made it to the bar and got a PBR. I felt the need for a break from Marc and Zelda, let them hang alone for a while. When the Bleeding Hearts started to play, the barroom crowd filtered into the showroom and left me with a seat. The bartender slid down to the end of the bar nearest the show and watched on. The guy next to me turned to me and asked if I was heading in to see the show. Nah, I'll wait a minute or two, I said. Yeah, he said. I'm waiting for the headliner myself. I hear good things about them, I said. You've never seen them, he asked. No, I hadn't. You're in for a good time. Apollo Sunshine rocks! That's what I hear, I said. Yeah, well they're pretty fucking good. I hope you're right, I said. I'm Noah, he said and reached out his hand for me to shake. I'm George, I said. We shook. You from around here, he asked. I live uptown, Washington Heights, I said. No shit, he exclaimed. I live in Spanish Harlem. Isn't that the other side of town, I asked. Well, yeah, but culturally it's a lot closer, he said. True enough, I said. It turned out that Noah worked at Mercury Lounge. He also worked at the Knitting Factory, and McCarren Park Pool in the summers. We talked all through the Bleeding Hearts' set. Noah is native to Ohio: Go Cleveland! He'd been living in the city for a couple of years. Yeah, I went to school Upstate, he said. He'd studied music and interpretive dance. One time we dropped shrooms and danced in front of like forty or fifty people for like twenty minutes. I didn't remember all the steps, but it was fucked up! He was insane. Giant beard and all. Noah bought a round of shots of Captain Morgan because his last name is Morgan and he thinks, after a few drinks, that it's a funny toast.

I told Noah about Marc and Zelda and he was interested in meeting them. It was less interesting and more difficult making our way back into the showroom. The crowd was thick. The Bleeding Hearts were on their last song. Zelda and Marc had disappeared. Masses of people clumping and moving excited and annoyed, liquored and drugged. I wasn't sure what might spring out of this environment, but I was curious to find out. Through this jungle of adorners we finally did bump into the two lovers perched betwixt each other's arms. I introduced them to Noah. Marc was looking lively and ready to see Apollo Sunshine. He and Noah got along. Apollo Sunshine started walking on the stage and Marc and Noah started going wild; I joined them. And Zelda joined us. Spots of people in the crowd overcome with calls and screams of exaltation. These guys were known around town. The lead singer smiles and he leans his head forward and you see he's balding on top. He starts the mic check again. And he looks at the other guys on stage who keep delivering more and more instruments to the edges and corners of the stage. And the lead singer is looking at them and smiling. He left the mic on the stand and walked over to one of the tables. He picked up a cowbell and showed it to the crowd in almost a threatening kind of way. Do ya wanna, do you really wanna see me HIT this cowbell? Oh, he hit the cowbell. And he kept hitting the cowbell. And behind that chiming entered a layered beat, hard on the drums. Bass boomed into the room and the guitar screamed with a motorcycle's roar. The man with the bell ringing overhead starts pacing around the microphone and talking, yelling words. I couldn't take my eyes off of them. I was watching a witchman of some woodland tribe perform a ritual and I was entranced. This ... this madness finally found its way into a rhythm and the singer into song. The bell and stick blasting erratically. He jolted from song away from the mic, put down the bell and started tearing off notes on a keyboard. Then he grabbed a guitar and bam, back to centerstage singing and wailing on the guitar and I'm like whoa. Noah's yelling over the crowd asking me what I think. I just yelled something. I'd been turned into some wild beast and it was awesome! Not a moshy kind of thing but people flailing, dancing. Wild, lost, gone mad in the wilderness, wrapped in mysticism and illusion. It was awesome.

By the time the Apollo Sunshine exited the stage, I was exhausted and wasted and sweating and horse. I was smiling when Noah and I went to the bar. Marc and Zelda hung back. It was as if they hadn't seen each other in a while. A lot of the patrons were leaving. There were other shows and afterparties and for others it was just the end of the night, something like one in the morning. Noah bought a lot of beers. He was looking for the band. Noah and I passed them some beers which they were glad to have. They said thanks. Noah started chatting them up about how he'd seen them before. I felt a little out of place just standing there sipping my beer, looking at the people milling around them, wanting to be near them. I was wondering how I was going to get home when I found myself in a cab, with Noah, on our way to Brooklyn to hang out with the band in Williamsburg at the Turkey's Nest. It was a little dive with quarter pool tables and beer served in styrofoam cups. I winced at the styrofoam, but grinned at the three dollar pricetag on the 24 ounce cup-o-beer. We popped some quarters in the pool tables and the juke box. We pushed some tables together. We breathed a second life into the bar that night and filled it with laughter, arguments about music and politics, Bush bashing as it were. I won two games of pool and lost one. I don't remember how I got home that morning, but I remember seeing the sun rise over the East river and the big city had not yet woke.

It was refreshing to be out on the those streets at that time of day. Many shops were still closed. The sidewalks revealed their true width. The air was chilling, the sun was bright, the bagels were warm and fresh. I picked them up around the corner from my apartment along with some fresh cream cheese with chives. At home I changed and sat and tore into my bagels and dipped them into the creamcheese. I turned on a movie and laid on my bed.

Chapter 16

The phone ringing on the floor near my
head woke me. It was dark outside my window.
Sam was on the line. There was a lot of noise
behind him. He was asking me where I was so I
asked him where he was. He was in a limo,
circling Time Square. What are you doing in a
limo, I asked. I'm drinking champagne, he said.
They were all there having a good time and
wondering where I was. They said they were
heading uptown, away from all the madness.
They were waiting in line to get on the West Side
Highway. They were coming to get me and take
me back downtown to join their burgeoning night.
 I scrambled to get ready, jumped in the
shower and slapped on some clothes. All the time
I was wondering where we'd be going. I imagined
all these classy places that I saw in movies and
magazine ads.
 The limo was lined in red velvet and Jarvis
was hanging out of the sunroof with a glass of
champagne and a cigar. At the same time, Sam is

trying to introduce me to this local legend. He'd come up in previous conversations. Jammin' Jarvis Wrightly only played with the most talented and respected musicians in New York. He'd even been recorded. Jarvis wasn't terribly interested in meeting me until we got to our destination. That's when he noticed I was there. He called me *the chap we picked up in the Heights*. He asked me what I played. He was shocked when I told him I didn't play. He looked incredulously at his friends when I said it. And then he looked at me suspiciously. Who was this person who invaded his special circle of musicians, his eyes asked. I'm sure that mine didn't have an answer.

Sam's long arms enveloped us all and ushered us away from the car, toward a door that I would describe as ominous. It was an old metal door at the bottom of a set of stairs, the type that might lead to a cellar door. Sam knocked, Shave and a Hair Cut. A big rectangular peephole slid opened and looked us over before opening. Eiden This was the gatekeeper of the Turkish Lounge. A large, good humored young guy that Suley had grown up with and who joined Suley on his international journeys just as soon as he was released from mandatory service in the Turkish military.

It was a hookah bar. No one was there other than Eiden's friend, Cash, who lingered on the edge of a display case. He wore dark sunglasses and stood stoic. He was very much part of the room's ornate décor. Our group – Sam, Alice, Charles, Joe, Kidd, Jarvis, Richey and myself – came to include Eiden and Cash. Cash didn't say much. He'd smile and laugh and then his face would go blank again. He said nothing, added nothing. He simply was. I wondered if he was a Buddhist or a Mime. I think he was on drugs. He was a strange character whom most didn't notice at all. Alice certainly didn't. I remember her laughing at something that Richey said. It was something that Sam had a rebuttal for and I remember laughing too. Eiden brought over three hookahs. They each had a different flavored tobacco. One was chocolate. Jarvis demanded it. One was Mango. I love mango. The other was Jasmine.

Along with the laughter that echoed on the rug adorned walls of this mysteriously smokey bar, came the zithers and song of Turkish recordings. And Martinis. There are so many different kinds of Martini. I didn't realize. I ended up with a Sapphire Martini with two olives. It was probably flammable. The olives were necessary to offset the taste of the alcohol, Juniper berries. All the same, I finished the first one fast and the next round came quick. The last thing I remember about that night at the hookah bar were the Martinis and the smoke ring contest. But then again, the memories of a whole new dimension to that night kind of dominate in my mind. It was the night the wall slid open. The back part of a sidewall in the hookah bar opened into what they called, The Turkish Lounge. Cash didn't seem at all shocked.

Like Alice Through the Looking Glass, we were transported from one world to another with only a few steps. It truly was a portal. Everything in The Turkish Lounge was designed to be visually stunning and texturally enticing. Vivid colors everywhere, though the room was not bright. Emerald greens and sun yellow. Crimson reds tracing. Purples. The people there were musicians and business people. They were artists and patrons of any and all genres and categories. But Sam and Jarvis and our gang were among the favorite of the many talents in the room. Favorite to Suleyman, the owner. His friend and business partner, Erman, was casually tending bar. I love it, man, he said. I don't have to do it. I run this place. But it's fun, man. He offered me a scotch, but I declined for a bottle of water.

Suley was a big Jazz fan from childhood and Sam and Jarvis were roundly recognized as two of the best Jazz musicians alive in New York City. Neither of them had recorded in a headlining album, but both have recorded with some of the more commercial musicians in town. I once asked Sam why he didn't record more often and why he never recorded a solo album. He shrugged and smiled and looked me in the eye. Life is good, he said. And he didn't say anything else on the subject. We weren't sober at the time and I didn't think it necessary to ask a follow up question. I can only guess that what he meant was that his life was, at that sparkling moment in time, just as he had wanted it to be. He neither needed nor wanted anything more.

Cushions. I've never sat on cushions like these before. I haven't ever even seen one like it since. The Turkish Lounge succeeded, in my opinion, to be the most comfortable place on the planet. You could not find a rough edge in it. No chair I have ever sat back on has caressed me in such a way, held me, comforted and supported me. I was on my second bottle of water and Erman looked at me and made a joke, what is he trying to sober up? You're in the wrong place for that, man, he said. There was a roaring of laughter through our group and all I could say was that I was drunk. Those Martinis destroyed me. I can't drink anymore, but I'm thirsty.

There were belly dancers, I shit you not. Purple and green sequence shimmering and those tiny cymbals on their fingers, chiming. I couldn't grasp the way they moved their hips.

Erman returned with a Shirley Temple and gave it to me with a big laugh. I laughed along. It was a good joke and it was super tasty. I asked him if he spiked it and I laughed. He looked at me real, real serious and said, what kind of place do you think this is? I looked at him. I could feel my face go blank, my jaw – slack. I don't know what kind of place this is, I said. But I like it. A roar of laughter through the strands of our group and the lime light was taken off of me. I was left with a befuddled feeling of total isolation from discomfort.

I watched Jarvis. He didn't like me. I respected that. Honestly. Who was I? An outsider. A nobody. What was I up to? Nothin', just riding along. Taking advantage? Sharing moments. He smoked a thin blunt out of an ivory cigarette holder. His suit jacket was a very dark purple. He was a class act whether he was a musician or a conman. I had a feeling he was a bit of each. He had an English accent that came in and went out of reception with varying volumes and inflections. He had big gold rings and patent leather shoes. He looked comfortable, lavish. I wondered what it was like to be him.

Suley came and sat down by me with a long sigh. Arms outstretched on the textiles. Satisfaction swimming in the pools of his green eyes. He was a tall, thin, graceful man. His movements were only deliberate and often exaggerated. The shift of his presence was smooth yet noticeable. He didn't look at me when he spoke to me. George, he said. His voice didn't boom or break into other conversations at our table. He lightly placed his sherry glass down on the low table. He smiled at the taste of it. He leaned into the cushion of the couch as if he were going to enter it. How do you like my place, he asked. Anything I could say would be an understatement, I said. In the positive, he asked. Of course, I sighed. He smiled. His head tilted slightly forward and the corners of his eyes lifted as he smiled. His head leaned back and he looked down his nose around the room as if to say, yes, this is my kingdom.

Suley and I got to talking in a casual sort of way. He was another one like Jarvis, flashy. But in more of an Eastern way. He didn't do the whole suit and tie thing like Jarvis and Erman. That night he was enveloped in emerald green. His shoes were slippers. His clothes were silk. He wore a full-length robe like a dinner jacket. He was the Turkish answer to Hugh Hefner. When I told that to Suley, he laughed and laughed and sent Erman for a bottle of water. Erman in turn asked one of the waitresses to get Suley a bottle of water. Suley opened the water, still laughing, sipped it and placed the bottle next to his sherry. He then took a calm sip of sherry, still smiling. It wasn't until this moment that Suley actually looked me in the eyes and I wondered if I were in trouble, but he was smiling and said that did I know that Hugh had been here a few nights before. He and Suleyman had a serious conversation about getting their two kingdoms together for the world's most grandiose party, but Suley was uncertain that that party would ever materialize.

Suley assured me, that though his options were many, he was no playboy. As if she could detect that her one true love was summoning her by speaking the syllables of her name, Hondai appeared. She was Suley's true female counterpart. Tall and graceful, waist length straight black hair, olive skin. She leaned in and touched her lips to his and sat serious and comfortable. Suley introduced us and she gave me her hand and I wondered if I should kiss it, but I just held it for a moment and looked at her eyes. She asked us what we'd been talking about. Suley smiled at me and then at her and said that we had been talking about her. She smiled, no wonder my ears were burning, she said. And in a sudden wave we were no longer small factions breaking off and connecting, but a group as a whole. Hondai introduced the topic of pleasure in physical manifestation as a question. The different boggling individual ideas of pleasure ranged from standing in the warm sun naked in a gentle breeze to the most rigorous sex to simple and appreciated companionship.

It was through the passageways of this conversation that we arrived at not the conclusion, but the inclusion of the drink that all my companions referred to only as 'the round'. I was not initially told what the round was. I was told that it was not alcohol. But I was warned that it was intoxicating.

After all that water, my buzz from the martinis was lessening. I weighed the option. No one hung over me or bothered me about it. My companions drinks came and they were drank as anything else. Most important in my decision making process; I noticed that the mood of the group lifted again to a new height. It was done without fervor, without mania or madness. It was done with a crisp comfort. I agreed to join in the revelry. Suley caught my eye when the waitress came with my drink and we touched glasses and drank.

When I was a kid, my mom took me to see the Disney movie, Dumbo. I knew the story by then. Mom read it to me. Then I read it for myself. But it was the movie that really stirred me. It was the scene of Dumbo, after drinking from the wooden kegs behind the circus tent. When he saw the dancing pink and purple elephants. I asked Mom what was in those crates. She said that it was ale. Not ginger ale, mind you, but 'grown-up' ale. I've had IPAs, ambers and stouts but they never brought me to what kind of state I felt Dumbo was in. The round did.

The toilet. It was a very nice, spacious throne that I found myself vomiting in. I kept thinking of the bathroom attendant. He was standing out there in his tuxedo holding warm towels and waiting for tips. I was really going to have to tip him after this. I kept hoping I wasn't making him sick. All the same, when it was through, when my stomach was empty and it stopped heaving. I felt pretty good. I washed my face in the sink and took a mint and a warm towel and tipped that guy well.

My high settled in on me. It wasn't a drunk. It was a high. The round has no alcohol in it. But it is intoxicating. 'The round' was a sort of nickname for one of the oldest pharmaceutical potions of human history, laudanum. The Mesopotamians, the Greeks, the Persians, the Romans, the ancient Chinese, the Celts, had all experienced the sensation I was experiencing.

Both medicine and recreation. Both poison and healing potion. Pain reliever and enslaving master.

Erman said, and I quote, 'We don't use no fucking blender, man. We're old school'. There were two ways that laudanum was made in ancient times and those are the two ways that the round was made at The Turkish Lounge. I had never known anything about any of this stuff before I came to New York and met the Turks and the musicians. It was delivered to me in an eloquent way which leads me to believe that it was either Suley or Jarvis who laid it down for me. Man, that shit really blurs together. It's just funny what sticks. Opium. I think: China, Tea, England, India, Pakistan, Afghanistan, Iraq, United States of America, Germany, France, Belgium, Holland, Japan, until I've hit every single country on the planet. Which is pretty much what opium has done. Opium crushed or opium sliced open and bled. All that sticky, milky white toxin separated from its shell and contained. Then mixed. With either red wine, or water and honey. So there were four different concoctions available at The Turkish Lounge: crushed and red/ bled and red/ crushed with milk and honey/ bled with milk and honey.

Any way you have it, man, you're getting fucked up, Erman said. His laughter haunts me sometimes. Just the way his mouth opened and bore his teeth, that crazy smile. I wasn't afraid of Erman. I got along well with him. Maybe it was the things he would laugh about that scared me. I don't know.

The first round I had. It was red and bled and I didn't know what to think of it as I held it up in my hand. A cluster of glasses held up toward the center of our circle and then, bam, slammed, down the hatch! And there I go. Into the, who? The, what? Into the, I don't know. And I pulled into the softest cushion of my body. Everything touch and everything smell was, hello darling. Love. Black poison that made dying feel good. I felt so good and I didn't notice anything else. Time was silky sand between my fingers. It was the texture of the pillows.

They lifted me up. I don't know who exactly they were. It could have been Charles and Joe. Could have even been Erman and Eiden. I felt terrible to be moved. They can tell. They tell me it's going to be good. They tell me they're bringing me some place special. My feet are moving beneath me. I can feel slightly my weight on my soles. Every step there is cushion on the floor. It's plush. It's smooth. Jesus, I think it's thick Chinese silk!

They set me gently on a big ass pillow on the floor in another room. We all had these lily pads. And I smiled and laughed. I felt sick and I swallowed. Then I started to feel self conscious. I looked around. My vision was a little bleary. I found near me a bottle of water and I was happy to have it. I drank and it emptied quick. Alice was talking with Sam and Jarvis, Hondai and Suley. Erman was chatting up Joe and Charles, Kidd and Richey. That's when I decided to make my way to a bathroom. Where the hell was there a bathroom? I tapped somebody's elbow and asked – in a sloppy way – I made it to the bathroom. The porter. I wished the porter wasn't there. But I was glad that no one else was there. I rushed the stall and I didn't have time to shut the door behind me. God, I didn't know whose ass had been there last. But hey, I was busy emptying my stomach the fast way.

I felt far more human and able to balance myself on the way back to the party. I better appreciated the carpet and more clearly understood the geography of the place. They'd only moved the group a room over, maybe three hundred feet. I sat back down with a smile. A cocktail waitress came over with a bottle of water. You're back to life, man, Erman laughed when I sat down. It was all good cheer and I smiled and laughed, happy to have that sick feeling gone. Still feeling good, but not to the height from which I'd just been dropped.

Joe came over, extracted himself from the comfort of his group in full social time. He sat down next to me. He had something real on his mind. Something intense. He was frayed and excited. He started talking about drums, about music, past sets. His toes started moving around in his shoes. His fingers worked in a beat. His eyebrows started jerking up, up, up as if they were trying to yank him off of the floor and toward that shining gold drumset within view. And while I'm zoning out and thinking all this, he's rattling on about the history of the drums in war and in music and the symbolisms. Techno music, I'm tellin' ya. I'm tellin' ya, they're prophesizing some insane future war … maybe Armageddon, Joe was ranting wildly. Frighteningly intense and then – a jerk into a smooth vibration, a total intensity plateau. In which space he rationalized his fear of

being made obsolete by a drumbox. High tech
beat machines … everywhere! I can keep up; and
I'm real, he said. He laughed and when he
laughed he let it all out: the anxiety, anger, joy. He
stood up from the bottoms of his feet and placed a
hand on my shoulder. You ever hear an M16, he
asked. I just looked at him. It was too strange a
question to answer quickly. I got sidetracked with
the thought of movies I'd seen. I'd been hunting
before, though I didn't kill anything. I'd gone to a
gun range once. I grew up in a red state. There
were guns around. I wondered if I'd seen an M-16,
certainly in some movie, Rambo or something. So
yeah. I finally answered in the affirmative. You
wanna hear one now, he asked. You have a gun
on you, I asked him. He smiled like the Devil at
me. Then he walked away. He was in a loose strut
and knew where he was going. I wasn't the only
other person to notice. Suleyman cheered.
Everyone else in sight followed suit. I cheered. I
had no idea what was going to happen. I was
given the biggest clue and it slipped on by.
Because I, along with everyone, it seemed, was
caught off guard by the barrage of imaginary
bullets barreling out in every direction from the
golden drumset and a lunatic smile! Then the big

man stood up. He wasn't jarred. He was steady and calm. It was Charles. He took his time finding his case. He took his time opening it. He took his time pulling out that gorgeous maple freestanding bass. He carried it slowly and carefully, only a few feet away from the machine gun fire.

The look on Charles' face was that of obligation. He sighed before he touched that first string. He commanded a few low B flats. Then he turned and looked Joe in the face until Joe made eye contact. They connected in some way and made an understanding. During this telepathic/psychopathic moment, Joe is still ramming out that beat and Charles is upping his tempo exponentially. Charles starts blending notes and dancing between the strings. He's battling Joe and matching him, keeping up with him. They'd formed an incohesive and unsustainable beat. But they went on. And then a confusion. The pin had been pulled. The timer, gone off. Wick, burned and gone. Silence followed. We were all lost, dumbfounded and half-deaf.

Charles eased the silence with a solemn note. Joe waved an apologetic wand over his symbols that seemed almost to cry. What lunacy,

I thought. What madness! Talk about swing ... from one end of the emotional spectrum to the other. They went off on a steady beat for a while and built upon it softly. In all, they looked lost.

Their shepherd came in the form of a woman. She was unusual. She was also mystically familiar. I thought of my accident. Such a jarring moment must have happened by design. Any cataclysmic event, whether it effect many or one. Or even two... Her hair swept down to cover half of her face as she leaned to open her guitar case. She had a Fender Stratocaster. A real beautiful guitar. She pulled the strap over her thin shoulders and cradled it comfortably. This made her happy. She looked down at the instrument and brushed her hair behind her ear and she smiled. There was an innocent beauty in her face. Something divine, in the traditional meaning, as if she knew something of or about peace and love.

She took hold of her guitar. She gently slid her long fingers up its neck. Silently, along the strings until she found her fingering. She let out a note that only a Fender could deliver. She smiled again and looked up at all of us and everyone was watching her. The microphone looked natural in front of her. She said, hi. She smiled and showed teeth. She took my breath away. Every innocent and purposeful curve of her face. The softness of her cheeks. The elegant shape of her eyes. I was captivated by her presence and a tightness in my chest. She played with delicate focus. She had rhythm. She had style. And when she sang, she sang with a heavy heart. It was the blues, baby! And her voice was all Sarah Vaughn. Deep and soft. A tantalizing mystery. I felt like I should do something. I never felt like that before. Do what, I begged myself. Something. She just reached into the deepest, darkest parts of me and started swirling everything around. What the hell! Stop. Stop singing. Stop calling me to you! I do not know how to approach you. I don't know when. And I don't know why I should even try. But I knew I had to, beyond any doubt. It was all I could do not to interrupt her playing.

My mouth was dry. I had no water. I felt no patience. I stood up and left and walked to the bar where the bartender was annoyed to be drawn away from her song. I just wanted a bottle of water. He slid me a bottle and I thanked him. I stood at the bar, farther from her than I was, and I sipped and I watched her and I sipped and I thought. I thought about the way I felt and then the way she looked and the way she sang and the presence of her and its effect on me. I thought of my mother and I dropped my bottle of water and snapped out of it and bent down and picked it up. Not all had spilled. Shit, I said. I grabbed some paper napkins from the bar and caught the eye of the bartender who grabbed my arm and touched my shoulder and smiled. He said, we have people for that. A young boy in suit pants and a vest came and cleaned up my spill. I poured the rest of the bottle into a glass and ran my fingers through my hair. I felt detached from myself, in a separate self, governing myself. But that just turned into dizziness. So I convinced myself that between the alcohol and the laudanum, it was probably time to go home. I lifted up my glass and tossed it back. When I put it down, she was standing in front of me with a smile on her face looking me dead in the eyes. The look on my face. She should have been able to read it like a child's book with big block lettering. But she didn't seem to see my emotions at all. Hi, I said. She looked happy, a little cautious, but she almost seemed as drawn to me as I was to her. Why did you get up, she asked. What, I asked back. She wanted to know why I

moved away from her while she was performing.
I told her I was thirsty. You must have been pretty
thirsty, huh, she asked. I asked her what her name
was. She was something else, really something
else. She smiled and looked down and let that
curtain of hair fall down. She lifted her head again
and made shy eye contact and shook my hand and
introduced herself as Kiesha. And then she slid
away into the rebirth of the night. There, inside
the Turkish Lounge. She seemed to just disappear
as abruptly as she'd appeared.

   Who the hell is that girl? Sam had
stumbled upon me at the very moment the blues
singer had vanished. I looked at him. He read my
face with literary precision. What happened to
you, he said. But it didn't sound like a question. It
almost sounded like he said, oh shit, she's got a
hold of you already. Forget about her. Come on.
He led me. You still got some night life in you,
right, he asked. My mind was not wholly with me
and I do not know that I answered as we entered a
much deeper reaching room. The colors of the
patterns on the walls and the ceilings and the
floors grew dark and veiny. A thin, soft hallway
opened. It was lit by an array of long-stemmed
candles posted high on the walls in decorative

holders. Red on darker red, plush motley floors and veined walls and ceilings. I felt like I was in something alive. In the far reaches of the large room, there were kneeling alters. Waiting in attendance were multiples of the well dressed boy who cleaned my spill. Sam had an arm around me as well as Alice. He was smiling honestly and it calmed me. His calm reassured me that I would be able to handle whatever it was that would come next.

Sule was the leading attendant in this pho-religious ceremony. Among the boys, at Suley's will, the first presented a freshly budded poppy flower that was shown to us up close as we knelt comfortably at these long, thin, bone-looking tables. One long thin instrument was presented and placed in front of each of us. It was not a musical instrument, but what looked like high quality chopsticks that had been hollowed out into straws. They were glossy black and each had a red dragon in a different pose painted on the side. Mine had its claws facing itself with thumbs facing out and chin up. Then came what looked like miniature tables, much like the ones we were kneeling at. They were slightly darker, but otherwise, comparable. Then the tiniest hibachi grills I've ever seen. Then a thin and very small piece of some kind of metal ... I don't know – silvery like nickel, but darker, almost blacked out chrome. I hadn't noticed until they lined up in front of us, but there were as many boys as there were attendants. They scooped into palm sized Santa Clause bags with little cinch ropes. They had tiny spoons with long handles. They placed a small mound on the metal plates atop the grills. I just stared at mine. It was all so terrifying, yet tantalizing. When the smoke rose, Suley instructed, breathe the smoke in with the straw. We could adjust our grills and even cut them off cold. Out of the dust, the ash, burning on this hot plate, a dragon arose. It was a moody white smoke. I inhaled it through the chopstick straw. My head flew up a thousand miles and lingered. I leaned back ... away from the table and onto the floor. So, so soft. The backs of my wrists, the outer reaches of my cheek; my shoes had been stolen.

I forgot all about my shoes for a while and let my eyes roll back. I wondered at how wonderful air felt in my lungs. I thanked the floor audibly, though softly, for being so accommodating. I felt good. I felt confident and happy. And then I found a nagging urge to go back to the altar. The boy had turned off the grill. I was happy that all that powder hadn't burned away; I was also irritated to have to wait for it to heat up again. Joe said something to me. I must have looked kind of tense. He smiled. He was sweating, a drop forming at his chin. It's why they call it chasing the dragon, he said. It always gets away from you. Then you're back here, waiting for the Phoenix to rise out of the ash, or dust as the case may be. I thought it was a dragon, I interrupted. His smile grew. Smoke is mutable. The Phoenix rises out of the ashes and transforms into the dragon. Sounds like a bunch of bullshit to me, I said and laughed, and I laughed loud enough to draw attention which made Joe howl. Our laughter, it seemed, ushered the response of the emerging dragon. Through my dragon straw, a flowing stream of woven, thin strands of smoke started to resemble the dragon on my straw ~ looking up into the straw and raising its claws as it stretched into thin disappearing wisps.

I leaned back on my hands. Joe looked at me. A girl was rubbing his shoulders. He started running his hands across the floor. There are thousands of nerve endings in each of your palms, he said. And on the bottoms of your feet. He reached down and took off his socks. He didn't have shoes either. Something was amiss, I could feel it. Joe starts intermittently and systematically rubbing the palms of his hands and souls of his feet on the floor. I leaned over to him and whispered my suspicion: I think somebody stole my shoes. Probably one of those boys. They look all good and innocent, but they're dope-peddlers, I said. Joe's face cracked slowly into a smile that spread like a crack in a windshield until it shattered into gregarious laughter. You jackass, he said. You took off your shoes when you came in. He laughed and fell back into the arms of the girl rubbing his shoulders and they tumbled and laughed and kissed and laughed and he pointed at me and they got up and walked away. I knelt and waited and smoked and splayed out on the floor in snow angel position. I made pretend snow angels for a while. Then I passed out.

Chapter 17

I woke up in my bed with no recollection of how I'd gotten there. It was kind of nice. I didn't have to wait for a subway train. I didn't have to pay for a cab. Just ... look at that, I'm home. I wish I could do it at will.

It's natural for my mind to go through its inventory of the recent past. I guess that it usually happens unnoticed in the mornings. Or maybe I just don't want to think about it and so shove it aside in my mind. But on this particular morning, I took some interest in walking through that inventory. Maybe I was trying to figure out what happened and how it happened; did I want it to happen again? If so, how could I encourage it? If not, how to avoid?

I was in no mood to rush. Not my thoughts or decisions. I wasn't about to move too quickly about my apartment or through my day either. Thank God for Sundays. They aren't what they used to be, but that is fine with me. Most of my life. That is, my life before college. My life under my parents' roof. Sunday was another day to wake up early. Sunday mornings I had to look extra nice. Nicer than for school. According to my mother, we were going to visit God Himself. It had the same feeling as when I was very young and we went to visit my dying Great Grandparents. I didn't know they were dying until they finally did. The way I viewed the world changed upon their death. That's what church made me feel for a while. But then it just slipped into being this thing, this place where people made sure they were all doing the same things in the same ways. They were concerned and careful. They were good people, are good people. But I didn't want to be what I saw as stuck. Stuck in this one frame of thought.

No, this Sunday didn't wake me up early. It didn't rush me into the shower, into suit pants, out the door and on my knees. I pulled on some sleeping pants and a t-shirt and took a cup of yogurt out of the fridge and sat on the couch and turned on daytime tv and kept the volume low. I made it through the yogurt and through the first part of the night, into the hookah lounge. That took me to a comfortable mid-afternoon shower, shaved, brushed my teeth. Then I felt awake and

clean. That shower took me to Keisha. I had no
thought or memory of her all that morning until I
was soaking in the down pouring stream of warm
water, the scent of soap all around me. All of my
other thoughts silenced when she walked into my
head, as if I had focused my mind for the first time.
I remembered everything I knew about her. Her
height, her shape, her voice, her smell, her smile,
her eyes, her. My arms stopped moving, my hand
stopped holding the soap. My jaw slackened and
my eyes closed. It was just her and the black
emptiness of my mind. No thoughts accompanied.
My attention was not divided. In my mind, I
watched her and waited for her to speak, to sing,
to move. Then I felt a deep swing of emotion. My
chest swelled. My eyes watered. I never expected
to feel this way. My throat felt tight and a little
soar. Then, all the little crevices in my emotional
body started to fill and warm and flow. I don't
know how long the smile was on my face before I
noticed it. But it was a huge, irrepressible smile.
And the word passed softly through my lips,
Keisha. Then I sighed and I felt a peace so pure
that I thought I had died. Then a force of air into
my lungs assured life. Things were happening
inside me that I didn't understand and could not

control. I started to feel pure and whole and good.
I have not felt like this before. I didn't ever want
to feel anything else. But a practical voice pushed
forward in my head. It said to pick up the soap,
finish washing and get out of the shower. The rest
of my day was dedicated to necessity: cooking,
cleaning, relaxation.

Mrs. Nims stopped by without warning. I
opened the door and smiled. She started talking
immediately and walked in passed me. I didn't
catch what she was saying. The last few hours had
passed quietly with me and I wasn't ready for a
rush of chatter. I offered her a glass of orange
juice. She declined. I poured a glass for myself.
She was rushing from room to room with a critical
glance. She found me standing in the center of the
living room sipping my OJ. She smiled. She
seemed a ball of nerves. She said that Mr. Nims
had been worrying that I wasn't taking care of the
apartment.

I wasn't ashamed of my living quarters.
My mother had always been very strict about
tidiness. Though it would be a little insane to be as
tidy as Mom. Mrs. Nims slowed down again and
sat on the couch and sighed. The place looks good,
she said. Mr. Nims is a crazy man sometime. I

offered her a glass of orange juice. She took it this time. You a good boy, ain't you, George. On the surface, I am. I try to be. But certainly not always. I wasn't coming on to Mrs. Nims. She'd just caught me in a contemplative space and her asking me if I was good agreed with the line of questions that had been forming in my mind, post shower. Which were essentially – what kind of person am I? Do I deserve love? Am I capable of receiving or giving real love? Was I, after such a brief moment, falling in love with Keisha? I'm afraid I wasn't very good company to Mrs. Nims. I couldn't say that I was all that present with her. I understood that she was there to fulfill an obligation to her husband and I respected that. Though I know a landlord has to give their tenant something like a week notice, I decided not to bring it up. I had nothing to hide and she'd been so nice. She soon stood up and headed for the door. I asked her to give me a little forewarning before she dropped by again. I said, please. She smiled and said I was a good boy and left.

Good in comparison to what, I asked myself. I have not always done what was right or good. I do not find myself to be special in that respect. There were things I wanted. They were things I was willing to work for, a career, money, comfortable survival … the American Dream. I don't think I deserved any of those things. But I hoped that if I worked hard for them, they would come. I still feel that way. But love. I had experienced closeness with people that bordered what might be called love. But what Keisha had suddenly filled me with was true and pure, fulfilling and potent. My initial reaction was that I didn't deserve it. I've fucked up every romantic relationship I've ever had. I've pushed away and been pushed away. My passion turns to anger. Consistently. My parents' relationship left plenty to be desired. And I'd never been certain if I ever wanted what I understood as love, especially when it transmutes into marriage.

At twenty-four years old, I knew people my age with rings on their fingers and babes in arms. I knew I wasn't ready for any of that. But I wanted to be ready to feel what I was feeling, because it was there; I was feeling it. Ready or not. I didn't know which way it would come. Would I find myself approaching her? Would she approach me? Would fate deal a hand in which we couldn't escape each other? Or would we pass like two ships in the night? I wondered if I even wanted to

have these feelings. It was distracting. I wasn't
sure what any pursuit might entail or even lead to.

Chapter 18

It wasn't until Monday morning that I
started thinking about the end of my night at The
Turkish Lounge and the laudanum and the opium.
I wondered if I'd gone too far. I got paranoid that I
might be found out at work, or that my
performance would suffer. I brought in a large
coffee with me and nursed it through the morning.
I didn't say much to Marc and he didn't seem to
mind. I did feel a little strange. I think it was
some lingering after effect of the drugs or the
booze.

There was nothing extraordinary about my
weekday life. My work was only mildly
rewarding. It was the possibility of where this job
might lead that I appreciated. The job itself, it was
tedious and a strain on the eyes. My body had to
exercise patience; it had to embrace stillness. I
found it hard to sit still sometimes. Other times,
the end of my day would come and I'd feel as
though my body had become too complacent. I
would walk home. Through the high

neighborhoods, through neighborhoods with bad reputations. Fear rarely crept up on me. Curiosity was my walking companion. I'd go home and look up apartments on Craig's List because I wanted a better idea of what these apartments looked like on the inside. I wanted a glimpse into the lives and living spaces of my urban neighbors.

In the mornings, I was sure to wake up early. But I have never been able to eat a proper breakfast. My stomach just does not want food in the first hours of being awake. Halfway to lunchtime, that is when hunger hits me. Some days I was prepared with a snack. Other days I would suffer until lunch. The amazing thing about lunchtime in this city is the array of options for food. Some days I ate Chinese food, others – Japanese, Greek, Polish, Thai, Italian, some days were burger days with French fries, and still others there was Creole. It was amazing. Where I grew up, I was used to American food: burgers, mac and cheese and sometimes steak, steamed veggies. My maternal grandmother was there and cooked heavy Polish and Irish foods, so much cabbage. It was a big deal to go out and have Italian food or Red Lobster. In college, of course, it was a popular thing to eat sushi. That was an interesting new eating experience and I enjoy sushi. But lunchtime in the office was truly a cultural experience for me. I was delighted when I found a Turkish menu in the office. I smiled and thought of the Turks at The Turkish Lounge. I ate a simple dish that day. It's a lot like Greek food, I think. There's pita and meat and hummus and vegetables. It was warm and healthy, comforting food.

Other than my walks home, I started doing push-ups, in the mornings, to combat the joy of lunch time. I know that it sounds very militaristic if you aren't accustomed to doing push-ups. And that thought can be very intimidating. But after you realize the work you are doing and the rewards you gain, it is easy to put that thought aside. Push-ups became the great confidence builder in my life. My arms slimmed and defined. My chest grew. My shoulders became sturdier. Twenty push-ups a day turned into fifty. Fifty led to one hundred and that is where I stayed. A hundred push-ups first thing in the morning is a hard practice to get used to. But my mattress was on the floor and it was no real fall. I'd roll, literally, out of bed and get my heart rate up. The good thing about doing this is that you snatch your workout without much consciousness.

You're done before you're mentally awake and it helps wake you up. I liked the way my clothes started to look on me. I liked the assuredness that I could catch myself if I fell, that I'd be able and well prepared to pick myself back up again. My daily push-ups became my daily prayers. They took my fears and frustrations and assured me that I would make it through another day, through the strange crowds and down the dark evening avenues. Less than one minute is all a set takes and it gives so much.

Chapter 19

Routine ate most of my weeks. The weekends didn't always bring excitement. They usually brought boredom and frustration. It piled up on the boredom and frustration I'd built up during the week. It would all heavily plateau on the top of my head. But the week that stands out next in my memory is the one preceding my first Halloween in New York City. Marc mentioned it to me in the beginning of the week. He even offered me to go out with them. He said that Zelda approved of me. A few days later, I woke up with a note slipped under my door, an invite to The Turkish Lounge for that same eve. Neither were requests I would decline.

Halloween. So much is expected of everyone in a holiday situation. I wasn't going to be the one to disappoint. At work, I hit the internet for ideas for a costume. I'd seen a Halloween shop just south of Union Square. I walked through it like it was a Halloween shop at the mall in Pennsylvania. I didn't see anything

that would set me in good style with the people I
would be surrounded by. I'd heard murmurs on
the streets about the sex shops on Christopher
Street. They were said to have some of the best
Halloween costumes in town. When I entered one
of these tawdry shops, I grinned. Those shameless
mannequins. Adorned with leather and feathers,
lace and whips and handcuffs and collars and
masks. I found a handmade leather mask,
something from, A Clockwork Orange and Eyes
Wide Shut. A hundred and twenty bucks. It
would be the centerpiece of my outfit. I found a
Salvation Army for the rest of my get-up: a nice
wool three piece suit. Late October being chilly, it
would all turn out well. I had a decent shirt and
tie at home. And a well-worn pair of soft leather
shoes.

Taking the subway had become a real
chore, but on this particular night, the subway was
a delightful freakshow. Colorful New York. With
bright colored costumes and real human
specimens hiding beneath them. Specimens of
what, I wasn't sure. But outwardly projected were
feathered pimps, and leggy prostitutes, sub-
humans, angels, vampires, superheroes, skeletons,
ghosts, little kids that were like midgets in all this

freakshow capsule sliding with speed in underground tunnels that carve out a prosperous and sadomasochistic city. Built up miles into the sky. The shadows and starlike lights that the buildings created had a special umbrella effect on this night. It brought us all together and sheltered us from the judgments up above.

At dusk on Christopher Street, I met Marc and Zelda in a little cutaway restaurant, a Mexican joint. I had a quesadilla. Marc and Zelda. Those two. Marc came dressed as … and I smiled when I saw him, V.O.I.D pasted on his forehead, with a madman haircut, his leather jacket openly displaying a marker scribble that I guessed Zelda wrote on his chest, You Make Me. He was Richard Hell. Zelda, she even had those nice curls. That short skirt with thick white stockings. She kept a copy of Save Me the Waltz with her that night. Zelda rolled her head back with a big smile and brought her chin into her shoulder and playfully said, 'I'm a flapper.' Marc and I both got a chuckle out of that one. It was all in good fun. But eventually they both turned to me with two questions. With their voices they asked what my outfit was. With their faces they had a little more attitude when asking, what the hell are you supposed to be? I smiled behind the mask that only covered my nose and eyes, the top of my face. They could see my grin. For all intents and purposes, I said, I am Mischief, but you can call me Robin, Robin Goodfellow. Marc laughed, but Zelda touched her face and mused vocally if I met the standards of the Puck character. There were two little leather horns sticking out of the top of my mask. It was a badass mask that stayed on my head with a leather strap. Should I have a flute, I asked her. You should have a flute, she said. But I don't know how to play the flute, I said and laughed.

From the relative order of the restaurant and into the chaos of the crowds awaiting the parade. The Halloween parade in NYC is no small thing, not for the party variety and that is some strange variety in this town. Early in the parade when the sun had just set, there were families. I was standing on a mid-rail on one of the scaffoldings and had a nice overarching view of the crowd of costumes and flesh. The peacocks and the skeletons came first. As the night became darker, so did the parade. Families shied away and the bold replaced them. Mardi Gras is for New Orleans. Halloween is for New York City.

All the masked debauchery that exists in this financial and about to falter town comes waltzing out onto the streets downtown and all across The Village.

The West Village, The East Village, Greenwich Village ~ the Jazz scene, the Punk scene, the Art Scene – The Village. It encompasses the Halloween Parade and my next two destinations for the night. But we couldn't miss the Grim Reaper marionette. It must have been thirteen feet tall. It was a spectacle. It took four much smaller, humanoid skeletons to command the puppet strings. But the night was wearing on and Zelda, running low in her flask, was eager to get to the Knitting Factory. I texted Noah as we walked down the misleading and meandering little streets. Noah made sure we didn't have to wait in line, but was sure to remind us to have our IDs out.

Punk Rock etched out a destructive capitalist market that was perfectly displayed by the Knitting Factory. The bars. Downstairs, way down stairs, sublevel, a beer bar. Twenty-three taps, from Smuttynose, to English IPA, Guinness, Blue Moon, Hefeweizen, etc. Upstairs, the plain bar with some topshelf like Kettle One and

114

Sapphire mixed in with Tom's bourbon and Old Granddad, though it did have Jameson. In the main showrooms, you could get anything from PBR to Corona to Johnny Walker to Jim Beam, and a cheap, cheap well. We each had a PBR and a shot of Jack. Noah took us back into a room where employees go sometimes and we smoked up with a bunch of people. It was good times. But Noah had to get back to work and there was a show we were there to see.

The Dwarves headlined. As it turns out, they're pretty much the best kind of act you could possibly have on a night like Halloween. Dark/angry music with the lead guitarist painted green and totally naked except for an Argentine wrestling mask. The guitar was the only thing keeping his modesty.

I stepped outside when my phone started buzzing in my pocket. It was Sam. They were heading over to Jules to play a set before going to the Turkish Lounge. It felt like a good time for me to leave. I found Marc and Zelda and I said goodnight. I ran into Noah on my way out and thanked him. Then out onto the street. Into Tribeca; Wall Street only a few steps away, but I was heading up from there. I caught a cab on the corner and watched the active city streets and its adventurous thrill seekers and amateur street performers acting out there personal nightmares against the steel, stone, and concrete of midnight here on this Halloween. A zombie jumped up against my window at a stop near first and first. It startled me. Where in hell was I?

I was pretty well tipsy when I got to Jules. But not that tipsy. The bartender remembered me and smiled and poured me a Duvel. I lifted my mask for the first time that night. I took a cool sip of the strong beer and set my glass on the table. Someone came from behind and pushed my mask down over my face and then stood in front of me so I could see her, it was Alice. Her hands held the edges of my mask and she smiled in an evil way at me and she kissed me on my mouth. I smiled and she walked away. I didn't know what that was about. I didn't put much thought into it. Sam sat down near me. He was asking about Alice. She took some pills and she's been acting strange all night, he said. She kissed me, I confessed. He shook his head. He reached into his pocket. He opened a small silver pillbox. He looked inside. He took out some pills and gave one to me. Go ahead, man, you'll feel good. You'll really feel good. Molly, he whispered and swallowed the pills. Molly, I asked and I swallowed the pill. It went down like Advil, candy coated. Get back on that water kick, Sam advised me. I finished my beer before I switched over to water. And somewhere in my drinking transition, Sam and Joe and Charles were on the little stage, blowing out the room. It being a dark colored night, Charles with the deeper tones of the bass gained a more prominent role than usual. Joe's wildman came out, dressed as John Bonham. Charles was doing his best Mingus with thin mustache, prominent goatee and beret. Sam spent so much energy blowing into his horn. He was too thin to be Charlie Parker. But he was serious enough to pull off John Coltrane.

Alice stepped on stage. She had a large presence for such a small woman. She appeared more on the eccentric side tonight and displayed her own subtle madness as Edith Piaf. She grasped the microphone as if it could feel her touch. She was feeling the drugs.

I started to feel the effects of the pill that I swallowed. My beer was finished and I was on a water kick. The cold sweat on the bottle chilled my hand in a way that made me take particular notice. My other hand rested on my knee and I started to notice the texture of my pants. A warm sensation blanketed my skin. I was breathing deeper than usual and it was a steady, calm breath. Oh, my god, I felt amazing.

Sitting at the bar, listening to them play – Alice's voice was particularly seductive. Charles's bass was bolder than I had remembered. And Joe settled back and played professional and reliable. Sam soothsaid a melody. I didn't know what to do with the strange, enticing feeling that I felt. I wanted to rub up against the bar like a cat. But I didn't. I didn't do anything out of the ordinary. I didn't act out my urges to touch and feel everything. I watched them play. I sat still. I sipped my water. I touched the fabric of my pants.

Alice cut her set early by fifteen minutes. She said thank you and walked off the stage and out of the place. She didn't look back. She didn't seem angry or out of sorts. She was done singing for the evening. I watched her leave. Charles and Joe watched her leave. Sam watched her leave. I had no way to begin to know what was going on with her this night and it was not my place to find out. Though I was hoping that that would end tonight's show. I had to get out of there. I had to stop sitting still. I was hoping we were going to the Turkish Lounge. Because if I was in a state of textile hypersensitivity, I wanted to be in a place lathered in silk and satin.

Sam was an ardent professional. He led his band to finish the set they came to play, the set they were paid to play. He didn't let the ecstasy interfere. He let his woman wander off without him. On this night, Sam aired his priorities. The band may or may not come first in his life. It was up there toward the top of the list ... with Alice. But number one on Sam's list of things that are important to him is his own reputation as a professional musician. I had no idea what was going on with Alice. Maybe it had something to do with coming in second in the heart of her man. Maybe it was something else entirely.

We found Alice at the Turkish Lounge about an hour after she abandoned Jules. She was wrapped in a shawl and sipping water out of a Martini glass and talking to Keisha. I met Erman at the bar and asked for a bottle of water. What is it with you and the fucking water, he asked. I'm on drugs, I told him. What kind of drugs, he asked. Molly, I told him. He smiled and slid me a small piece of chocolate. I popped it in my mouth and asked him, what do you know about Keisha? He smiled and turned his back to me and took a glass off the rack and a bottle of Dalmore off the shelf and poured himself two fingers. He drank half his glass in one sip. She's a singer-songwriter, he said. Yeah, I got that much, I said. If you want to know more, you should ask her, he said, but she's a dangerous woman. I would let curiosity lay on that subject, he said. Dangerous, I asked. In the way that women are dangerous, he said.

Something kept Erman from speaking much on the subject of the singer-songwriter. He led me away from the bar and into the deeper reaches of the lounge. A private setting for our particular group. It was a room lavished with pillows and lounge chairs. All the tactile wonders of the world. I kicked off my shoes with verve. I dropped my suit jacket on top of them. It was made clear that I was in a safe place where I might indulge in the wild desires that were influencing me. I soon found myself slipped comfortably under a chaise lounge and caressing a pillow. I was still feeling a little too reserved, or uptight, to strip down naked and slide my skin on every surface I could find. There were others in the room. It wasn't a solitary confinement. The room jiggled and moved with familiar faces floating about.

Two sets of stockinged legs barred themselves in front of me. I could smell their skin. It looked soft and smooth. The stockings made Xs patterned down their legs. Two legs disappeared as they crossed over the companion in the set. I could feel a bead of sweat move across my own skin. I touched my chest and popped a button from the top of my shirt. I slid out from under the chair and startled the two mystery girls. I apologized and started through the crowd of people to the other side of the room. With every elbow rub and shoulder brush I felt as I walked added to the friction that was building up inside of me. I made my way to the little bar in this room and asked for a bottle of water. I hadn't realized how hot and thirsty, how dripping with sweat I was. The bartender handed me a bottle of water. I popped the top off and chugged until it was gone.

The water was excellent. I placed the bottle softly on the bar and felt the urge to glance to my right. An empty seat between me and Keisha. It was a startling revelation. I sat down as quickly as I could without raising suspicion. Keisha, I said aloud and looked at the side of her face. She turned to me and I looked into her eyes. Like looking into the eyes of a mystic, I could not look away. The music in the room and the chatter silenced. All my peripheral vision blurred. There was nothing in that short moment but her. I'm George, I said. She smiled. Is that your name, she said. I laughed. Yeah, it is, I said. The room reappeared and a strong pressure was at my stomach. Excuse me, I said. I made my way to the bathroom and pissed out about a gallon of water. It just kept coming out. I washed my face and looked in the mirror. My pupils were saucers. I didn't blink for some time. I just stood there staring. The attendant woke me by handing me a towel and I dried off and moved on.

Joe caught me outside of the bathroom and put his arm around my neck and was talking and laughing and asking where in the hell I'd been hiding. I told him, under a chair. He howled and expressed his appreciation of my sense of humor. He dragged me over to the bar, but not the bar that Keisha was at. Joe was talking and I looked at him and I smiled. I liked Joe's company. I liked that he felt comfortable with me. I liked that he was wild and fun. But my mind kept traveling back to Keisha. I didn't know what I wanted to say to her, but I wanted to continue the conversation we had just barely started.

Bring your water with you, Joe said as he led me away from that bar. I wouldn't let myself do what I had the urge to do, namely fondle every texture in the room with every part of my body. And I couldn't think of what else I should do. Besides, I've trusted Joe before to no harm; I followed him again. I was hoping that I would run into Keisha.

We weren't heading to the room with the alters and I was glad about that. I couldn't handle any more drugs, nothing hard, at least. We climbed some steps up a carpeted spiral staircase. I could feel the bass in my chest. The lights flashing and moving in the darkness, the smell of designer perfumes and colognes. The people sweating and pulsing and dancing. Joe rubbed my back calmly and smiled at me. He could see the wild madness I had been containing beneath the surface. His face was all sympathy and understanding. He kissed me on the cheek and laughed and pushed me and hollered, go dance. I didn't know who in hell to dance with. I have always been a bit socially awkward. I saw an attractive girl not far and I listened for the rhythm of the beat. And I started to move. I positioned myself in front of her and danced a little. She was dancing, but not with me. I tried to make eye contact with her as if to say, is this alright with you. Clearly, it wasn't and she moved on.

I felt silly momentarily. But I ignored the slight chill that she'd left me with and I closed my eyes and I just listened to the music. I made like the music, like the beat itself was my dance partner. That wonderful warm feeling was alive inside of me and I smiled honestly and danced and sweated and moved. With each moment, with each song, my movements became freer and I melded with the music. One girl near me found herself alone and joined me. I opened my eyes and smiled at her. She looked at me as if to say, is this alright with you? And I smiled. Her hands touched my shoulders. I could smell the mix of her sweat and her perfume and it felt nice to not be dancing alone in a room packed with people. I let my hands touch her waist and we made it through a few songs. Before she left she kissed my cheek and whispered a thank you in my ear and I felt good. At that point I was wondering where my friends had gone and I glanced around the room. I saw Keisha dancing with someone. She was nice to look at. I watched her dance. She didn't look at him, the guy she was dancing with. When the song ended, she looked up at him and smiled. Her lips moved as if she'd spoken. I couldn't hear through the fog of music and didn't care to know. But I did care that she started to move away from him. I didn't even think before my feet started to move. I was making a bee-line to cut off her path. She was moving slowly, looking for the free rhythm of a suitable partner. I made my path so that I would meet her face to face. I slowed my stroll as I approached her. We made laser eye contact a few feet before I reached her and she stood still for moment, facing me. I was more forward than I knew I would be. I didn't stop approaching her until our noses almost touched. Our eyes never strayed from the other's gaze. There was a brief moment of stillness as we stood eye to eye. I gently rolled my hands onto her hips. She lavished my shoulders with her arms. We moved. Her body. My body. Anticipating movement, keeping with the rhythm. We made heat. I wanted to devour her. Slowly the space between us disappeared. I don't know if I kissed her of if she kissed me, but we had a hold of each other in a powerful way. The song ended, but we didn't stop. The next song came on as if the last had never ended. We swayed, we moved, intertwined, pulled and tore at each other with soft fire. My hands went from her hips to her back. They made their way over every socially acceptable place on her body. Textures of her silky dress and her hot skin. I remember her fingers making their way into the strands of my hair, down my neck and all about the socially acceptable places of my body. God I wanted to tear her apart, but in a good, kind, gentle way, but furiously.

After what must have been a few hours, my clothes moist, my legs sore, she stopped moving and pulled the scruff on my neck and pulled my ear to her lips. She said she was coming back. She was going to the bathroom. I didn't think that was such a bad idea. I found a men's room and released another gallon or so. When I looked in the mirror this time, I noticed that my pupils were returning to their natural state and I was starting to feel fatigued.

When I went back into the party, I noticed that the crowds had thinned considerably and I declined from looking at my phone for the time. The people left in the room where we were dancing were few and the energy was low. Even the DJ seemed to no longer care about the music and was talking to some girl, though a record was spinning. I recognized no faces in that room, no Keisha. I started to feel a headache coming on and I was glad to leave that room with its pounding bass.

Down the spiral stairs, into the room where I'd hid earlier under that chair, I found Erman sitting and talking with Charles. They welcomed me to sit with them and asked me how I was feeling. I shrugged my shoulders and asked the bartender for a bottle of water. He delivered. I scanned this room and didn't see Keisha. I excused myself from Erman and Charles's company and walked into yet another room and another room. Sule's place seemed to be a labyrinth of endless rooms. Room after room, there was no sign of her. I was running out of the very last of my energy. All I could feel other than the pain in my head was a tugging at my chest, a growing emptiness that became more and more apparent to me the longer I failed to find her. I didn't even have her phone number. No one would tell me anything about her. I would ask her anything and everything myself if I ever really could, but every time I saw her I was far too overwhelmed and intoxicated; I could never think in a logical, linear way that would lead to gaining information like: what's your phone number, or your last name.

I finally came to the room that would lead me to the outside world, the city streets where the sun's yoke was breaking on the pavement to burn away the retinas in my own head that had become accustomed to the lesser light of The Turkish Lounge. I wanted to bid farewell to someone before I left, but I wasn't about to wander back into the maze of rooms behind me. All was empty and quiet as if I'd somehow stayed when I should have been gone. I took a deep breath and pushed the door open to the outside world. I felt like an alien watching my feet fight for which one gets to be in front. I'd managed to remember to pick up my jacket and shoes. It had been an amazing night. I just wished that I wasn't walking with the terrible sinking feeling that I had lost something in the mix. A cab driver pulled his yellow car up next to me and opened the window. He asked me if I wanted a ride home. I got in the car and told the stranger where I lived.

Chapter 20

To this day, some five years later, there is an air of pain and mystery surrounding the events of the following Monday. How did it happen and who is responsible, really, the truth. Hidden. Apparent. I just remember standing in front of it. The clouds in the moody city parted with a halo above the wreckage. A sinking feeling in my stomach. An awareness of my smallness within the world became apparent to me that day. My breath didn't know what to do and it became nervous and erratic. My thoughts swirled and I couldn't catch any of them. Newspeak had fallen, been knocked over, knocked down, no more. My skin cooled and numbed. I closed my eyes. I couldn't look at it any more. Voices. Screams. Fire and smoke. I didn't know what to do. This is where I was supposed to be. In there. Sitting at a computer wondering if this job could take me where I had wanted to go. The computer was done, gone. The job was over. That path was erased.

A policeman directed me away from the site. Hoards and herds of people. I was one of them. We were led up through Columbus Circle. Everyone in the city -it seemed- was out on the streets. I tried to imagine what we looked like from above. I could hear the murmurs through the crowd: what would happen next; would something happen? There were screams of sheer terror all around me and inside of me. Fire trucks came and firemen and firewomen rushed out of them and into it, into it. The police … everywhere. Police cars and police trucks and tall horses. There were mysterious black cars with men in black suits carrying black guns. Men and women in business suits. Some wore the latest fashion while others wore the uniforms of their daily lives. We were all stuck there on the streets. I didn't even know if we were allowed to leave. Everyone just absorbed and reacted. Some people collapsed. People bursting into tears. I just looked around. We looked at each other's faces for some understanding, but everyone, everyone, was just astonished.

It was as if I slipped again into the dark, cold wetness of my unconscious. But this was alive and breathing. This scene was before me with no chance of waking into a different state. Something terrible had happened. My place of work, once a tower, a tall building that gave so many of us a daily refuge, a place to work. Now, a gaping hole, a heap of rubble. So many now gone, dead. I slept in fifteen minutes; I was late and so I am spared. The dust was still settling, grey snowflakes made of ash, floating on the gentle air. A sedative feeling came over me. My rush of adrenaline had passed. Everyone had been dusted gray as had the streets and the lower end of the park, grey trees almost bare of their leaves.

My immediate, debilitating reaction was over and I needed a place to sit. I had to get out of the crowd. My phone exploded with calls and texts. I turned it off and made my way around all the people. I started walking toward Union Square, a place that I simply found comfortable and comforting. It was a long walk. I didn't even want to know what this disaster did to the subways. I could feel blisters starting on my heels by the time I got to Union Square. Dress shoes. It was there on a lonely bench in the park that I pulled out my phone. I just looked at it for a minute before I turned it back on. I pressed the green button: Go. 32 voice mails. 88 texts. I never knew I was so popular. Mom was the first person I called: yes, of course I'm still alive, I'm on the phone aren't I? Yes, I am alive. It's a good thing to tell yourself. Go on, say it out loud. I am alive. Me, right here, living human being. I think. I feel. Hello. I am alive.

But were my coworkers? Were they still alive? I didn't even bother looking for them in the mess. A tragedy engulfed the city. I wasn't going to start asking, hey, have you seen Marc, or Harold, Michelle ... Audrey? I only knew their work numbers, their extensions. Except for Marc.

After I called everyone back, I called Marc. Yeah, I'm alive. I was going to quit today, he said. They showed me. I laughed. I'm sorry. It was funny. We met at the Coffee Shop, a trendy little bar in Union Square; I hear it's owned and run by supermodels. Marc ordered two rounds of some Brazilian drink. It was sweet and we drank slowly. He slumped over the bar and rested his head on his hand. It was funerary talk. And rightly so. And what are we going to do for work, he said. He swore he didn't care because he was going to quit anyway, but me ... he was suddenly very concerned about me. My guess: though he honestly wanted to, he wouldn't have quit. If the building were still standing, he'd still be working and complaining, but working. He along with me and all the other survivors were thrown asunder, left to feel guilty to be alive and completely oblivious to what our next move might be. Thank our lucky stars we're still alive, clink glasses, sip and smile at each other, guilt-riddled smiles of happiness and sorrow.

We got drunk that afternoon. We ended up in Little Italy looking for a slice and a place to relieve our bladders. You couldn't have told that we had met Tragedy earlier that day. We were falling down laughing and falling down drunk.

That was the last that I saw of Marc. Sure, we see each other on Facebook sometimes. Marc soon after moved to New Jersey to edit a small magazine. He was just across the river, but I only ever went to Jersey to visit Gram, and Marc never could bring himself to meet me for drinks in the City. It was a brief friendship that ended much as it began.

It was the next morning, or rather afternoon, that I woke up from the binge. I was in my bed. It was a weekday. A drill ran through my head and why was there always jackhammering? There is always jackhammering.

Can't a guy sleep off a hangover in relative peace without the jackhammering? I went to the bathroom and took a couple dry aspirin. This is when I felt my skin turn cold. No job. No money. No way to pay for the little that I owed. For some reason, I felt compelled to find Suleyman. For some reason I felt compelled.

I put on a good combination of clothes and hopped on a train downtown. When I arrived at his stoop, I took a breath. There was nothing to worry about. Suley and I are friends. If nothing else he will listen and understand. If nothing else he will be a friend. If nothing else … I was hoping he'd be able to help me out. That's what it was. I was there as a beggar. Please sir, tough times have fallen just as my place of business has fallen and I need an alternate way to pay. I have to pay or else end up on the streets. They aren't kind or gentle streets. I will not survive them.

Erman opened the door. He laughed when he saw me. He invited me inside. What can I do for you, man, he asked as we both sat in a well furnished room. This was not The Turkish Lounge. This was the townhouse adjoined, their townhouse as far as I know. I apologized to Erman. I told him about the magazine, about work

and what happened. He knew. He heard.
Tragedy. He poured two glasses of cognac and
handed one to me. We sat and talked and I told
him that I was worried about work and money
and hoped that he and Suley might be in a
position, somehow, to help me.

He smiled and I knew he needed time to
think. If something comes up, I asked, please
think of me. I will tell Suley, he said. I'm sure
there is something. If nothing else, keep looking.
Keep looking. I tried to smile at him. I shook his
hand. I left. Newspeak was my big break. Maybe
if I'd been there a year, maybe then I could enter
another magazine. But I'd barely made an
impression. I tried not to think of it, not then.

I walked for a while in uncomfortable
shoes. I found myself at Croxleys on First Street
and Avenue B. I ordered some hot wings and an
amber ale. Noah showed up and we got a booth;
they're old church pews. Noah did most of the
talking. I just tried not to think. I finished my beer
and wings. Noah ordered a pitcher. It could
always be worse, he said. I smiled. It's true.
Things can always get worse; it's Life's greatest
threat.

The pitchers flowed like carbonated wine. Tipsy turned to drunk and drunk got stupid, and stupid is so much fun. Ask your mom if you don't believe me. The light of day slipped below Manhattan's famous skyline. The dark came to mask our excessive drunk and Noah and I left the bar, spilled ourselves onto the sidewalk. I don't know what we were laughing about, but it was necessary laughter; the type that washes away an onslaught of sadness and despair.

Somewhere near Washington Square Park we picked up some water. There were all sorts of people in the park. A crowd. Someone was swordswallowing. Others were filming. Most were just sitting or milling around. A small group played old hippy songs on an out of tune acoustic guitar, and off key singing. Noah and I laughed at all of it, at this scene, at the neighborhood, at the city itself. It was all so absurd! This is all too bizarre. It's one of my favorite places in New York City. But that night, that night, it was all a joke.

Chapter 21

It was dark again when I woke up in bed. I'd slept through an entire day. My mouth was dry, my head ... pounding. Aspirin and water. The glow of the light in my kitchen was depressing. It reached out into the otherwise dark living room. I was standing, looking at it as if it were the failure of my life. There was a knock on my door. I was sure it was Mrs. Nims and I didn't want to answer it. I walked over to the door anyway and looked through the peephole. It was Erman. He was not alone. He had girls with him. I turned on the light near the door and opened it. He covered his mouth and started to howl. You look like shit, man, he said as he walked in passed me. The girls were giggling and looking at me funny.

What's with you, he asked. I told him that I just woke up. He made a comment about it. He sat on one of my couches and told me that I live like shit. That's a fucked up thing to say to somebody, I told him, even if it is true. The girls started dancing with each other and begged for music. I broke out my laptop and put on some jazz. They wanted club music. I don't have club music, I said. Not very NYC of me. What can you do? I'm me. I don't know who else to be. Erman laid out a thick line of coke for the girls and reached toward me for my computer. I'll find some music, he said; go take a shower.

I could hear them through the walls whilst in the shower. Thank God for water. Seriously. I'd heard that there was some Japanese doctor in Japan studying the healing nature of water. He has a strong thesis and his analysis is on a molecular level. But I don't know his name. This is all just some trivia I picked up on the subway via Columbia University students.

I put on some clothes before joining Erman and the girls in my living room. I thought it was a shame that among the women he could have brought to comfort me, why couldn't he have brought Keisha. On second thought, I was glad that he hadn't. I was in a terrible state. Erman was not entirely there to help. I sat down next to him on the couch. We were talking small and the girls were dancing for us. Erman could not get over the way that I lived. He thought only mental patients lived like this. Hey, I said, it's clean; I clean it. It's not a total dump. He laughed his frightening laugh.

Erman had downloaded some club music from the internet for the girls. He fed them fat lines of cocaine and it was fun watching them take their clothes off. He lit a joint. We did a couple lines. He pushed a needle under my skin and I watched in horror as my blood mingled into the syringe and that dark liquid disappeared into my arm. Heroin. Erman assured me that it was very good heroin. Don't get me wrong, I protested for a hot second. But a hot, naked girl that smelled of exotic beaches begged me and I start to lose track of my memory around that point. There is something ridiculous about heroin. It was a heavenly feeling and hell itself. I could feel myself turn into a piece of shit and I didn't care. Wonderful is not the word I would use. I couldn't move for a while. I saw the girls. They did things. I didn't care. I wasn't really in that room. I was just watching from another dimension.

I woke to Erman slapping me in the face. Come on, man; come on, George, it's time to go. I could hear the water running in my bathroom. The girls were taking a shower. I felt disgusting.

What had I done? What was I doing? What had I become? Of course, I didn't ask any of these questions aloud. I didn't want to offend my company.

I put up my hands to stop the slapping. I opened my eyes and I looked at him. I was still on the couch. My skin felt waxy and disgusting. Why are you slapping me, I asked. He handed me a glass of orange juice. It's time to start our day, he said; we have a big day ahead of us. After I took the glass, he pushed into my small bathroom and hurried the girls. George, go … take a shower. The girls were still in there when I disrobed and jumped in the shower. I asked him what I should wear. He said it didn't matter.

A limo was waiting for us outside. The girls were becoming bothersome. They were complaining. They were hungry. They were dissatisfied with the previous night's accommodations. They were roundly displeased. We dropped them off somewhere. We were both glad to be rid of them. I didn't know what they were all about anyway. It's all just part of the show, he said.

We stopped off at some place for breakfast. It was fancy and I felt underdressed in jeans and sneakers, a sweater with no undershirt. It was a vegan breakfast. He said it would be better not to have anything heavy since we did heroin the night before. I had a bunch of fruit and a cup of coffee and it felt lacking. I was still accustomed to eggs and bacon for breakfast.

Back in the limo, we did rails of coke. I don't know why. I was totally lost at this point. My personal American Dream had seemed shattered and if this new friend wanted to help me in the ways that he seemed to understand, I was willing to dive into the deep end.

We traveled up and down 5th Avenue. Armani Exchange, Barney's, Saks, Bergdorf's. It felt strange to me. He was buying me socks and suits and ties and shoes. Oh, my God, rich people are comfortable all the time. I could jog ten miles in the leather shoes he bought me and my feet would be fine. The fabrics of the suits felt like they weren't even there. I was forced to stare at myself in enormous mirrors and I looked like a bizillion dollars. Clerks were so nice to me. They hung off of me like Marc did Zelda. I didn't understand what it was all about and I hoped that Erman wasn't hoping to have sex with me. It wasn't going to happen. He read that thought on my face and he laughed at me. I don't swing that way, man. Don't start thinking crazy. But, oh, I told him, we passed crazy about six miles ago. He laughed that scary, crazy laugh. He started talking seriously. I had asked for a job from the Turks. My request was being granted. The night before had been a test. I showed no problem with serious drugs. I showed no prejudice against anything or anyone. I was open to whatever world presented itself to me. And that was the only kind of person who could be trusted. Suleyman, Erman told me, trusted me. He liked me. I was going to work for them. I was going to live well. I was going to do what I was told. I wondered, does something like this mean that I've sold my soul? Are these Turks the Devil? What kind of old school train of thought is that? It was bad; it was all bad and I knew it. I have to admit, I was kind of liking it. Our last stop was far from the yuppie shopping district and down on Soho's cobbled streets. I hope you know how to ride a scooter, Erman said to me. He put me on top of a brand new Vespa. He stroked his chin. It would be better if you were taller, he said. It'll have to do.

Erman instructed me to meet he and Suley back at the town house. He left me on the Vespa and he disappeared into the limo. I sat there for a minute revving the engine. I felt like I'd just gone through a storm. But it was one of those storms that comes back around and really gives you the business.

I revved the little scooter engine. The speedometer read up to 120MPH. I couldn't imagine. I'd have to find a real open stretch of straight road to feel anything close to safe to crack it wide open. I wondered if I should have a helmet. That probably coursed against the grain of the Turk's sense of style. I'd never ridden a scooter before. It seemed easy enough. No shifting. Just turn it on and twist the throttle. I checked my mirror for traffic. I looked over my shoulder to double check. The coast was clear. I started to go. It was a little scary at first and then suddenly liberating.

I got away from the cobble stone streets as quickly and carefully as I could. When I found my way to smooth pavement, I really started to get comfortable. This was really something. And to think, I had seriously been considering quitting, giving up, giving in, letting go my crazy dream. But crazy dreams need crazy friends and when those two elements come together the crazy doesn't seem so crazy. Somewhere in the folds of my subconscious there was a childhood voice that called, hey moron, what about the very real and terrible consequences to such a venture? What? Did you say something, Super-ego? I can't hear you. I'm way, way too busy having fun.

Chapter 22

I always thought that rich people were happy. And I'm not talking about what I first understood as wealthy, a small town doctor or even lawyer, the owner of a prosperous hardware store. I mean the inheritors of fortunes far beyond middle class comprehension. People who own buildings on Park Avenue, major investors in world markets, international decision makers. The puppet masters of whom we are all puppets even as we believe we make our own decisions and on a micro level we do. But it is the absurdly wealthy and terrifyingly powerful who splay out our buffet of mediocrity of which we all must accept. The alternatives are variations of poverty and death. But I didn't know until after some time in New York City that those born into great positions also sometimes choose poverty, death, slavery. These are the only places that heroin leads. Unless of course you are involved in its distribution and not its consumption.

I should have been guilt ridden. I should have been beside myself. Instead I ate veal and garlic creamed potatoes. I drank thirty year old wines. I slept on a three thousand dollar mattress and finally got a bed frame. I felt a debt to Mrs. Nims and honored our lease agreement and so stayed in that little apartment. I also knew that my new arrangement was tentative. But the money was rolling in, in waves. Like a Tsunami. Suleyman didn't pay me anything. I lived on tips. The pocket change of some of these people would make you gasp, even faint. The first time I was slipped a five hundred dollar bill, I smiled. But the last time, I didn't. I said my thank you and made my way.

If I were a smarter person, I would have been investing. I would have been saving. Instead, I saw it all as a twisted and fateful adventure. I could not account for any of this money. It was partially a simple gratitude to a dutiful servant and the rest was hush money. I had been invited into the foyers of apartments higher in the sky than peaks of modest mountains and as large as Hollywood mansions. I was sniffed by dogs who dined better than half our world's population. And my work was easy.

Scoot around Manhattan. No deliveries outside of the borough. Easy. Breezy. Often fun. The only real hassle of the job was not knowing when it would begin or end. I could be beckoned at three in the morning and I had to arrive. Interrupt a movie and I had to go. In the middle of breakfast, lunch, dinner. Anytime. And quickly. But I didn't mind. It gave me a false sense of importance. Like I were a high-profile emergency room doctor. It was all very inflating. I did enjoy this job.

After six months of working for Suley, I had five suits and six pairs of shoes. Their cost could bring half the city's homeless out of poverty for a good month or two. On Wednesdays the drycleaner came by to pick up my laundry. All hours of any day I raced through the streets on my little Vespa. I wore sunglasses all the time. Powerful people knew my name and since they could never admit to anyone that I was their drugdealer, I was occasionally introduced as the young writer, George Wordworthy.

The young writer. He lives in a well furnished but otherwise modest apartment in a questionable part of town. He pours himself two fingers in a rocks glass of sixteen year old scotch.

He got a new computer, Sony Vaio, something fancy and expensive. He doesn't know how to handle being pseudo-nouveau-riche. He thinks to himself what is worthy of the page. It is white. It glows a spray of white light into his otherwise dark room. He thinks of what he can do and sweats and he drinks. He thinks about Hemmingway, about Wordsworth, Shakespeare. He thinks about how he felt walking around the MET, looking at all the well preserved art.

It's all bullshit, I think to myself and take a sip. I light a cigarette. It's impossible. Everything really worth saying has already been said. And who the hell am I to think that I could say it any better? What experience do I have? How can I compare? I write a few words. I delete them. I take a sip. I light a smoke. When did I start smoking? It must have been in the last couple of months. I never smoked before, never even considered it. I didn't like the smell and didn't want it on me. It must be part of this new persona. What was I becoming? I paid a hundred dollars for a haircut. Two hundred on the sunglasses. I was losing myself in superficiality and materialism. I hadn't been to church in over a year. What about asceticism, I asked myself. What

would God think of what I am doing? God.
Fiction. Some long bearded grandfather in the sky.
What would he have me learn from this path I am
on? According to the prophet John Lennon there is
nothing I can do, nowhere I can be that isn't where
I'm meant to be. Lennon, McCartney, even the
other two. The last prophets I've heard of. They
visited the Dalai Lama; they spread their word
around the world and learned ever more as they
did. We as a society make little of them now.
They fathered a revolution of love. I once asked
my pastor what God was made out of. He told
me, love. I asked my western philosophy
professor in college what love was. He said it was
a chemical reaction that could be triggered by ten
pounds of chocolate, but usually interpersonal
psychic connection and sexual arousal. The
professor wanted me to realize that love, lust,
chocolate were all about the same and that reason
and technology were now the voice of God. My
pastor just wanted me to feel loved and belonging.
The professor wanted me to feel smart. I sat on my
high tech, ergonomic swivel chair and sipped my
aged scotch. Two fingers, three fingers, drunk. I
couldn't write. The drinking, the smoking didn't
help. That didn't mean I wanted to give up on

them. Maybe I should have set it all aside, accept poverty and regular work, learn how to meditate, go back to the church, be a mouthpiece for the Lord. Yeah, nobody wants to read that pedantic shit. Not these days. God no longer matters. The spirit is dead and the soul is myth. Just put the powder on the spoon, dissolve it in water, heat it, soak it into a piece of cloth, dry the cloth with a syringe. Shoot the only God you will ever know into your corroded veins and be with Him there in the Holy dimension of decay and chemical slavery. I understand it as far as I understand that one experience that Erman gave me. The sudden jolt of relaxation, of numbness, a subtle hint of ecstasy. I heard my heart slow. I saw the room shift as my eyes slid up and rolled to the back of my head. My skin cooled and then I was gone. In limbo. Nowhere. Through a portal into another dimension. But I never saw God. I didn't see the Devil either. There was nothing. No great lights. Just an emptiness that was somehow comforting until the high started to wear. Then a sickness that the marijuana helped to quell.

I considered trashing my room, breaking my mirror. Maybe even a window, but where is the point? What would that accomplish? My head was spinning. My depth perception was shot. I drank a glass of water and fell asleep on my bed with my clothes on.

Chapter 23

I ordered a limo to pick me up at The Turkish Lounge. I'd started spending less and less time there since I started working for the Turks. I was only ever really there to drop off cash and pick up dope. I'd had a long day. Twenty three deliveries all over Manhattan. It was a Friday night. I had two tickets to the theatre. I'd finally managed to get Keisha's number.

It wasn't the cash that I'd suddenly come in to. We had a real connection. She had a way of just letting me talk. It almost made me nervous. She met me one night at Le Petit Café. Well, before that … I ran into her on the street, on Thirty Forth Street. She had a weekly gig there, on Thursday nights. It was a small venue, a private club on the eighth floor of the Manhattan Center, where both the Grand Ballroom and Hammerstein Ballroom are. I was on my way to meet Sam and Alice. They were just finishing up a gig and I had been up all night delivering. She was in a group of about five people. I was on my scooter. There were some groups coming out of the Manhattan Center, the stage lights under the awning. I looked over and I saw her, unmistakably her. I hadn't seen her since that night at the Turkish Lounge, when we danced.

She didn't see me; I know she didn't. She wasn't even looking in my direction. This was my one real chance. I was sober. I was feeling good. I pulled off to the side of the road and shut off the scooter. They were walking briskly. I ran a few blocks to catch up. I was a little out of breath when I did catch up. I grabbed her hand and said hello. She was startled. The people in her group looked at me funny. I smiled at her and looked into her eyes. I wanted to see if she remembered me. It took her a second. Then she smiled. I don't want to keep you, I said. I'm on my way to meet some friends. She smiled again. It was a little past three in the morning. I took out my phone and got her number. I felt good about the whole scene. Sheer confidence. Nothing hindered me. I was where I was meant to be. It was fate.

I left her there on the street with all her friends. They were off to go finish their night and I had my own people to meet to do something about my own night. A few days later Keisha and I met at La Petit Café for coffee and tiramisu. We talked and laughed. We had so much in common. What was between us, what potentially bonded us was so much more than late nights and wild friends. She was a Jersey girl transplanted to Upstate New York before she came to the city. I was a Jersey boy transplanted to Pennsylvania. All the commotion of our lives mirrored the other. It was like looking at a still lake and seeing the sky above. When I was with her I felt lifted. I felt cured and pure and whole.

When we talked about music, it was a funny argument. We loved the same music for different reasons. She understood music from a mathematical perspective. The balance of the notes were all triangulations. A science as she understood made into art by way of constant application. She was a musician. She sang and played guitar and she understood each song as a story of sorts being told through the numerology of the notes that the mind understood sympathetically and unconsciously. I just like the way it sounds, I told her. And I wondered if she thought I was stupid for saying it, but if that's what she thought she did a good job at not showing it.

It made me smile to look at her face. She had charm and grace in all that she did. Even when she became nervous – I could see it in her hands first, confirmed by her eyes and hidden behind a confidence like marble, smooth and beautiful and strong. I felt a pride swell inside me at the few moments that I knew I made her nervous. She would demure. She had a long neck and slim shoulders. There was a simple elegance in her style. Her fingers were long and thin and cool to the touch. We smiled at each other when I touched her hands, when I held them to warm them, to warm her.

This night I bought us tickets to a raved Central Park play, As You Like It. It was Shakespeare in the Park. I had reservations at Tavern on the Green. Dinner, then theatre. She loves that kind of thing. All the New York savvy Hollywood A list would be in town during the weeks of Shakespeare in the park. Culkin, Streep, Malkovich, were in town and I heard they were all going to be there this night.

She looked beautiful when I picked her up. She was wearing the dress I'd bought her only a week before. She smiled and was smiling. She radiated and her radiation melted my heart and I knew I was a fool for her. I was happy to be. I was so happy. So relaxed. Beyond anywhere I'd hoped to ever be.

Chapter 24

As far as I was concerned, I was living a life of intrigue. A double life. I told my family that I got a job at The Village Noise after Newspeak was destroyed. They were happy for me and asked to see my articles. I demured. I played cool. I told them it was an entry level position behind the scenes and without credit. Assistant to an editor is what I told them. They never came to visit me in the city so they never saw my fancy post modern furniture, my pillowtopped California king, my lavish wardrobe.

In a way I had become one of those tourists that I'd envied when I first got to the city. I didn't wear an I heart NYC shirt or anything. But I bought a painting down in Soho. I ate brunch in French restaurants. I once took Keisha to dinner on top of the Empire State Building. We went for a horse and carriage ride one night. I took limos instead of cabs and left the subways to those who needed them. I sat in lavish corners of exclusive night clubs. This Big Apple had become my jeweled oyster.

Winter had come and riding the Vespa had become an unreasonable act. Suleyman arranged for me a Towncar and constant driver. It made Noah look at me sideways. I told him the truth when he asked what I was up to. He disapproved of the way that I dressed, of the lifestyle I'd taken on. He said it had no integrity. He called me a sellout and laughed. I paid for our drinks. He wasn't mean or course. He didn't even mean to be rude. He was just being honest. He thought that struggle was important. He was worried I was losing my artistic integrity. That made me laugh. I didn't know that you or anyone else considered me an artist, I said. You were an aspiring writer when I met you, he said. I told him that I still was. But when he asked what I'd been working on, I had to admit that there was nothing. There was no work in progress, no signs of artistry of any kind. I hadn't written a word. I'd just been out working and having fun.

Noah really struck a chord in me that night. It got subtly under my skin and by the time I was comfortably at home and getting ready for sleep, I was irritated. At first I tried to ignore it. But this irritation … it was a self irritation. It was me. I was losing my Self somewhere in all this excitement. I was leaving my Self. I knew this situation wasn't going to last; it was just a little fun and adventure in the midst of this experiment that was my journey into Urban life.

I couldn't sleep. I couldn't get comfortable which is ridiculous! I had one of the best mattresses that money can buy. I got out of bed and turned on the light. I turned on my computer. I made myself a cup of tea. I checked my email. I pulled up a blank word document. I just started stringing sentences together. Just write, I told myself. It doesn't matter if it's any good. Just write. Just get something down. Remind yourself of your typing skills … at the very least. Reacquaint yourself with the written word. Try to remember what you learned in school. Try to remember Milton and Shakespeare. Try to remember Hemmingway and Plath.

I wrote one garbage sentence after the next. I filled up a page and I kept going. I drank that cup of tea and made myself another. I sat and sipped and put words down. They were nothing special words and I'm not sure what I was trying to say, but I do know what I was trying to accomplish.

I started to remember why I came to this town and money had nothing to do with it. It was all about experience. I came here for the city itself. I came to be a part of this crazy town. I wanted to find the magic and the insanity, to make sense of it, write about it and become a part of it. At least for a little while.

Around morning I started to see that I was becoming a part of this city. Granted, not the best part. But I was integrating. I was experiencing. It was time to start writing and understanding. I knew then that I had to start rearranging some of my priorities. I had become too indulgent. I never cooked for myself anymore. I always ate out or ordered in. I didn't want to change that. But maybe order in more than eat out. I needed to spend more time at my computer. Winter was perfect for this … it's not like I was going to want to go on a lot of long walks.

The sun started to break into my apartment and I started reading through what I'd spent the whole night writing. Ten single spaced pages of gibberish. It was mostly introspection. Nothing anyone else would bother reading. As I read through it, I hardly wanted to read it. It was painfully unveiled and openly confused. But I had committed to the act of writing. Get something down; just get anything down, a professor once told me. You may never write anything publishable, she said to me, but at least you will know that you are a writer. It was deprecating encouragement, but encouragement. She said it in a way, with wavered voice, that made me think there was some kind of bravery involved as well. Or maybe she was just nuts; you know what they say about English teachers. Which is why I never want to become one, not because other people would think I'm crazy … I just don't actually want to become crazy.

 I didn't get any sleep at all that night. I got ready for my day when the sun was fully up and I left the apartment to pick up at The Turkish Lounge. There was some holdup and I got stuck sitting around for about an hour. It was fine with me. It wasn't a very lucid day, I wasn't entirely with it. I felt introspective and started remembering the story of my life in New York. It was short lived at that point, but it was lived. I knew there were stories within. I even knew what a few of them were, but how to get them out properly, I wasn't sure.

I was lucky that I didn't have to drive myself. I couldn't pay attention to anything going on around me. The driver knew where the drop points were and told me when to get out. What's wrong with you today, he asked me in a believable Pakistani accent; ever since I met Jarvis I started questioning all the accents in the city. I told him I didn't sleep well the night before. He said that it happens to him every once in a while. He offered me some sleeping pills in case it happened again; he suggested that I get a prescription of my own: they're easy to get, he said; just tell your doctor what happened. They give them out like candy.

Pills. Pills for sleeping, for depression, for anxiety, for confidence, for your skin, your heart, for pain, for relaxation, for enjoyment. The whole damn world is self medicating and I'm supposed to believe that I'm a bad guy for delivering heroin? Maybe I should go get a medical doctorate and then go back to peddling heroin. It's been used medically worldwide in one era or another. It's ridiculous. My theory is that in fifty years medical science is going to be all apologetic when it finds out that all these everyday bullshit drugs are destroying people's livers and giving them cancer. But the profiteers will sit back and say, what can we do – the damage is already done. They will be fat and well clothed and totally comfortable. How am I any worse than them? Tell me that. I didn't share any of this with Mohammad, the Pakistani driver. He thought I was out of my mind. He kept giving me strange looks through the rearview mirror. What's your problem, Mohammad, I asked. Are you taking that stuff you deliver, he asked. No, why do I look that bad, I said. You look like shit, George, he said. You look like shit, you towel-head motherfucker, I said. That was the last straw with Mohammad. He stopped the car in the middle of the road and pulled me out. He pushed me up against it and punched me in the face. He called me a heathen, as if anyone in this world isn't. I took a swing at him, but landed face down on the dirty concrete. I was trained in the Pakistani military, you fucking asshole, he said. And there I lay, face down in the middle of the road with an ounce of heroin and five grand in cash on my person. I watched the car drive off. I was having a bad day.

I got up and brushed myself off. I walked back to The Turkish Lounge and told Erman what happened. I told him I was sorry. I told him I was out of line. I told him I was sorry. Oh, yes; I was sorry, the sorriest sack of shit around as far as I felt that day. I couldn't believe the way I acted. Very uncharacteristic. Something was getting to me. I think I was freaking out.

Erman took me home in his personal car. We sat in the back of his Bentley. He lit a joint and we shared it. He said the bad days happen and that I'd been a good employee. He said that he was getting a bunch of people together that night. Sam and Alice and Joe and Charles were going to be there. Keisha had agreed to come. He said that I should go to sleep for the rest of the day and go out with them that night. I didn't really feel like it. I didn't feel like doing anything at all. But it was an interesting tone that he had in his voice, a tone that told me I would be a fool to miss out. He said he'd swing by well into the night to pick me up.

Get some rest and stop insulting the help, he laughed that crazy, scary laugh. I smiled at him and waved and walked inside. I ate. I slept. I didn't think too hard.

Chapter 25

En Medias Res … into the action, a party in Harlem. All the pomp and festivity of the nineteen twenties except showing a little ankle isn't taboo. The walls sweated and breathed and I was sober except for the martini I was nursing. I'd learned a little something about martinis: just because they go down easy doesn't mean you should drink them like water.

There was some tension. I was hoping that there wouldn't be a fight, but it was looking grim. Luckily the hostess, Mme. Williams was as seductive as she was large and she was a woman of many dimensions, not unnoticed by many of her young, male attendants. She seemed to burst out of every seam. She was a lecherous delight. I personally enjoyed her presence as an extrovert, a sexually charged woman, not shy, openly forward, and a woman who would not put up with any shenanigans in her home.

Luckily, I was far from the crosshairs of her seduction. But with the company I kept, I was well within the warmth of her charm and good graces. It was a party of musicians, for musicians. Brass and strings and percussion. A DJ was mixing up a beat and playing along with the *real* musicians. Bud Powell was on the piano and mixing it up with anyone who dared. And there grew the tension. Powell was a strange guy, a real passive aggressive genius. There was no one around with any knowledge of music that didn't admit in one tone or another that Bud was a genius. But he was far too temperamental and unpredictable for his own good. In this case, on this particular eve, he was set on playing the piano. I don't think he has either interest or skill in socializing. He had all his life, as far as I've heard, only ever been invited to a party as part of the entertainment. It was the only role that he knew, enjoyed, wanted. As long as he was in a party and there was a piano, that piano becomes his one and only social partner.

He played beautifully. He mixed in with the DJs, with the various guitar players, drummers, trumpeters, saxophonists, clarinet players; there were so many musicians. And they were all there to play with the famous Bud Powell … whether they knew it or not, whether they liked it or not. This had upset someone. I saw him. I along with everyone was looking at him. They had made a scene. Here, in Madame Williams' house in Harlem. She was yelling. She was bouncing. Bud had his knife drawn, already having stabbed this man once in the leg. The man was standing, bleeding, screaming and waving his arms. Powell sat on the piano bench, knife drawn, blood dripping. I wasn't sure how to feel, but I was entertained. Sam stepped in. His arms went around Mme. Williams and the bleeding man. The three of them disappeared into the numbers of the crowd. Silence formed momentarily. Bud placed his sodden knife on the piano and went back to playing. An acoustic guitar strummed in behind. DJ supplied the beat. I wondered if this would start something negative with Joe. That energy was in the air. But nothing more to that night. I ate some Mac and Cheese. Mme. Williams had made enough for an army. Chicken too.

Somewhere in this sordid mess, the curtains fall; they fall on me anyway. These curtains becomes the backdrop for Keisha and myself. A little theatre in BK. The Williamsburg Players. It was a small stage in a stone room. Folding chairs. A friend of hers was in this 'neo-traditionalist, atheist extravaganza', as The Noise reviewed it. I didn't care. There was electricity between us. We could have been seeing a children's play or at one of those old time porno movie theaters, like in Taxi Driver.

I was to witness nothing quite so grotesque. The neo-traditionalist, atheist extravaganza, or To Have Not, was a love story. The Players wrote it out together. They were a strange bunch of hyper-educated actors. They were addicted to the stage, as one of them said afterward. We went out with them for drinks.

I just wanted to make out, but it was important to Keisha that we were there for her friends. We were doing something good, supporting the arts and all. I warmed her hand and she smiled at me. I watched her. The lights went on, on stage. Keisha's dress showed her thin, expressive shoulders, her long neck. She caught me looking and pointed my chin to the stage.

It was a dark comedy. A forlorn love. The background favored the colors of the boroughs. The leading actress, Keisha's friend, Margo, in black and purple. Jack, the leading man, in black and red. They were all vampire sheik, if you will. It wasn't a vampire story, but they never ate and there were no mirrors. But no one got bitten and no one was killed. It was interesting. It lasted an hour. Like a Lutheran day of Church. We never really did call it 'mass'.

I think that there is something religious about theater. Call it the theater of man, whereas church would be the theater of God. Just as the battlefield is the theater of war. And as the great playwright has said, that our everyday lives are but a stage and we individually, the players. The theater is a symbol of humanity as a civilization. It was a little too heavy for the feelings of the night. They were suspicious, searching for a sarcasm in my voice, but there was none. I don't really like it as a medium of communication. Not any more, at least. I've exited my moody teenage years and I do not lament them.

The makeup was off and the cheers were on. It was a little Irish pub around the corner from the theater. It was packed and popular. A little stifling, but the company was interesting and extroverted. They were open in discussing their strategies for creating their characters and criticism came in crashing waves followed by calming laughter. Keisha was happy, laughing – I loved you guys, she said. They attacked her like a pack of lapdogs begging for a treat. Each demanding their tid bit of encouragement and a taste of her compliments.

She appealed to each one of them, but Keisha is no liar. Which meant of course that handing out praise went easier with her for some of her friends than others. But she found at least one perfect little compliment for each of them. I sat back and sipped a beer. I was a little bleary, happy, but not totally drunk. I liked watching her. She was perfect here. She was showing so much. Remember, it is usually she who shyly basks in the limelight of an evening. Here, no one treated her as if she were any kind of star, no one but me. But at that moment, she was happy with my silence.

I smiled quietly for an hour or so, sipping slow on not too many beers. Our limo was waiting around the corner. The driver tirelessly in his seat listening to late night talk radio. We stood out in front of the bar for another forty minutes saying goodbye. At this point I was consciously applying my patience, but I didn't let my minor annoyance show through my face or my posture. They laughed and kissed cheeks and complimented and flattered and fawned. I was so happy to sit in relative silence in the car for a moment. The soft leather seats eased my irritation. And then Keisha thanked me herself. She thanked me for my patience, my attendance, me. She showed me so gently and so powerfully her happiness with me. I was happy to be hers'.

Chapter 26

I went back to work after a couple of days
to myself. I partied and socialized but I didn't
spend any time at home writing. I spent the day
with Mohammad. I bought him a small gift and
apologized for my previous behavior. He said he
forgave me, but we didn't say much to each other
after that. We went through the day and made our
deliveries. But the whole day I was introspective
and disconcerted.

After the last scheduled delivery of the day,
I went to The Turkish Lounge. I gave Erman the
money. He counted it out and we talked small but
I was as distracted with him as I was with
everyone that day. What's with you, George, he
asked. I asked about Suleyman. I wanted to talk
to him. I wasn't sure what about, but it was
important. We sat down together. He offered me
some tea. He was in the townhouse, away from
the raucous of The Lounge. He asked me what the
matter was. I told him that I wasn't sure. He
laughed a little and we sat there in calm, quiet

company. I sipped and tried to explain. He
sipped and tried to listen. I was talking about my
writing. It used to be the most important thing to
me. It brought me here, to this city. It took me to
college. It got me through high school. I couldn't
just leave it for the security of a job, not even for
the warmth of a woman. I told him that I felt lost,
separated from the me that I knew. I needed
inspiration and concentration. I needed to know
that I had some time during every day to sit at my
computer and write. No matter what went down
on the page. I thanked him for the job and all the
fun and money that it brought me. It gave me the
ability to give Keisha so many good times. It gave
me the wonder, the tickets to see and be a part of
the city that I so wanted to discover. But I had to
write about it. And I couldn't write, couldn't
concentrate knowing that I could be interrupted at
any moment and be called away to work.

Suley looked at me like we'd been friends
all our lives. He sipped his steaming tea
contemplatively. He took a deep breath and he
smiled at me. He recited my name and let it hang
in the air, George. He was working on some
thought. I waited patiently. I hadn't asked him
for anything. I simply told him my pickle. He was

searching through the inventory of his mind for the right words to accompany the thoughts brewing within. I silently thanked his diligence. He was so careful with his words I might have thought he was a master poet. I don't remember verbatim what he said and I am not myself a master poet. But his words were warm; they were a friendly embrace. I don't understand what he saw when he looked at me. I don't understand why this particular friend wanted to spread his generosity my way, but he had with such consistency it was almost hard for me to be surprised at the meaning of his words. He asked me to take a break from work. He said that Mohammad could handle the deliveries until Spring thawed the city. You must have a substantial amount of money laying around, he said. Enough to cover your modest rent until -say- May. Until then, I was invited -more clearly- insisted upon to stay in his townhouse, his modest Lower East Side mansion, until I produced something publishable. At that point I would resume my role as the delivery person of The Turkish Lounge.

Chapter 27

I dreamt of an expansive African landscape with broad swaths of sparse grasslands and scattered low rising, broad limbed trees. I was laying on my back staring off into the horizon, clouds whisked and spooned throughout the crystalline sky. Two thousand shades of blue. I breathed through my long nose. The warm air filled my lungs and I stretched from toe to toe, across my long body. I was laying in the shade of one of the sporadically placed low rising, broad limbed trees. I licked a paw and brushed the hair away from my face and yawned. I rolled on the floor of my hunting grounds and wakened my senses.

I stood and closed my eyes and pulled my head back and stretched out my neck. I leaned low forward and stretched out my front legs. I opened my hips and stretched out my hind legs. I scanned the terrain, my terrain, and picked a direction. My legs moved me with fierce power. My lungs pumped like a combustion engine. The faster I ran, the sharper my vision, the more sensitive my sense of smell. And then suddenly an aromatic perfume. I slowed my pace and turned my head in the direction of the scent. I glimpsed something and slowed ever more.

I focused my eyes with predator's precision. Before the form registered in my mind, the millions of hairs across my entire body stood on end and shook me. I lowered my head and squinted hard against the intense sun. She was only a silhouette. I only saw the outline of her curves, her long, lithe legs; the graceful curve of her smooth neck and slim shoulders. She moved as if gravity was but a polite assistant aiding her graceful return to Earth with each long stride and nimble leap. She was still for a moment. Her head turned, but with the distance between us I couldn't tell if she turned toward or away from me. I closed my eyes again and caught her scent again on the subtle breeze. I let her aroma cycle and circle through the long passages of my nose and tasted the air she floated on.

I stalked toward her, but not directly at her. I didn't want to make my presence known. I didn't want to alarm her, to scare her away. I traveled a jagged path and made a mystery of both my presence and my intentions. The sun shined into my face before it slipped below the horizon and I hoped that my position was not made apparent to her. Under the camouflage of night, I moved more comfortably. I stalked her scent and paid more attention to the sound of my paws patting the ground than I did the image I cast across the plains.

The night grew long and the air cooled. I found a small patch of grass, large enough to lay on. I rested. My muscles were hot and tender. I covered a lot of land. But she was close by. I allowed myself to sink into sleep until the sun once again touched the horizon. A hunger had grown strong within me. She was not far, but she was already on the move. She must have started just before dawn. She must have been on to me. Either that or she had a far off destination. Probably, she was catching up with her family. It is rare to see a gazelle off on her own, away from a larger group. She must have gotten lost during an earlier predator attack, probably a leopard. Who knows. Who cares. I found her and I would have her. I was sure of it.

She was fast. I started a steady run and caught her scent. She was moving faster than me.

I was losing her. The landscape was changing. I hadn't eaten in over one day and the rate I was spending energy, I would surely fall flat on my face if I didn't figure something out soon. At this point I was losing my reasoning abilities. I caught a strong waft of her scent. She must have stopped somewhere for a rest and I felt a surge of energy. Hope filled me. I was catching up with her. In the midst of my renewed hope, I passed up the offerings of smaller and less desirable meals. Animals that hadn't noticed me until I was upon them. I heard a heart or two stop as I passed, but I wasn't interested in these insufficient snacks.

I was starting to realize that I was outside my home ground. I had left my kingdom to catch her. I had entered some other lion's kingdom. A cardinal law broken. It sent a surge of concern down my spine, but I was fortified and ready for any confrontation. That beautiful creature that I spied during the setting sun, she was mine and I was ready to cross any land, through any kingdom to claim her.

What started as open plains, my kingdom, turned to a place less open, more lush. Trees grew in number and grew in height and closeness. The grass beneath my paws was thicker. The sun became sparser. Songs of birds filled the air. I could hear the scurrying of small animals all around, hiding from me. There were creatures I had never seen before. A long, legless animal hissed in a branch. It sent a terrible sensation through my body and quickened me through the trickier trails that I traveled. The aroma of the foliage made it harder for me to follow her by smell. I scanned for her more strongly with my eyes, but I couldn't see her. I listened for her, but it was a noisy place that I found myself.

My senses were being overloaded and I was losing my prey and my confidence, my assuredness. I hadn't lost a prey since my mother taught me how to hunt. I was the best hunter of my brothers and sisters. I was the strongest, fiercest and most feared lion in my kingdom. Lions that crossed into my domain had learned from their own spilled blood to stay out and my kingdom grew by bounds as I reached maturity. How had such a lion found himself so lost? How had *I* been outwitted by an herbivore? I was growing a noticeable irritation.

I felt a sudden urge to stop. I stopped running. I stopped chasing. I breathed and felt the warmth of my blood surging under my skin. I was feeling tired, but that's not why I stopped. It was a clearing in the forest. The trees formed a line and stopped. In the clearing, among the still lushness of the grass and flowers, a perfume lifted in the air. There was a lake, a large, long lake that I didn't see the end of. There is where I saw her. She couldn't run forever, just as I was learning along my travels that I could neither run forever. I was glad to stop and catch my breath. She stood among other gazelles, drinking from and bathing in the lake. It was easy for me to recognize her in the crowd. Her form, her spirit seemed to call to me. As I gazed into the group, she stuck out to me as if she were an altogether different species though they were all gazelles.

I laid myself on the soft cool grass for the first time since I entered the forest. It was a softer bed than I was used to. I laid my head on my paw in front of me. I watched her. Her graceful movements. Her balance. Her calm. The line of her neck as she dipped her nose in the water to drink. A surge and a leap. Her entire body was a sight that I could lay my eyes upon for hours.

What could it have been that lead, that let a lion fall in love with a gazelle? I didn't have a wife, no children. I hadn't mated. This feeling I felt, it was the first time, and it was an experience. I closed my eyes for a moment, keeping track of her smell to know if she were leaving. I closed my eyes and imagined in my mind what it would be like if I were a gazelle. It would make this position I was in so much simpler, or at least easier on my emotions. I would be a strong gazelle because I am a strong lion. I would have the grace of a gazelle. Perhaps not as graceful as she, but enough to show her that I would be a good mate. I would show off for her. I would give gifts to her. I would mate with her. Our family would grow from there. We would eat leaves and berries and run together and play games in the water.

Poetry played in my mind as if some ancient human were standing behind me with a lyre. But anger permeated my emotional landscape and water came to my eyes. I opened them and rested my watery eyes upon her and kept them open to dry in the moist air. My anger came from my knowledge, knowing that my fantasy was nothing more. I forgot my fantasy and lost myself in watching her. There were a few more hours in the day. I wanted to wait; I wanted to prolong this inevitability of nature and the hierarchy of the grasslands. I know this is the forest, but the forest isn't so different from the grasslands that I should act any differently than I knew I would.

She had caught up with her family. She was young, but mature. She approached an older couple that must have been her parents. They embraced each other, holding their heads close and almost entwining their necks. Then she went off to a group of younger gazelles and played games. I hadn't played like that since I was a cub. It isn't appropriate for grown lions to frolic.

I spent hours laying in the shade watching her, ignoring my thirst and hunger. But the day wore on and the end was nearing. I stood and closed my eyes and pulled my head back and stretched out my neck. I leaned low forward and stretched out my front legs. I opened my hips and stretched out my hind legs. I scanned the open space and peered down the tree line. My strategy formed and I knew what to do next. I moved slowly, but with the assuredness I had grown into, the certainness in the hunt of a lion. I am a lion. I am a lion on the hunt and she is my prey. She is mine and I will make it so. I stalked just behind the tree line until I found the perfect spot. And I emerged from the bush into the open valley and built steadily up to full speed. It took a moment for the herd of gazelle to sense my presence. They scattered, but I had her scent; I had her in sight and I did not let my eyes off of her. I worshipped her as she fled me, but I had the jump on her. She no longer had a chance. The sense of security that her kin gave her was false. If she wanted freedom and liberty, if she wanted to live past her beautiful prime, she should have kept running when she caught up to them.

  I leapt and sliced into her flank just before she made another bold leap. I knocked her sideways but she did not fall. She slowed and I was able to grab onto her from behind and drag her down to the Earth. I pinned her there and no gazelle on this gorgeous planet is brave enough to even attempt to save her from the fate that had been cast upon her. My hind legs stood atop hers. My forepaws pushed her lovely neck to the ground. I looked into her deep brown eyes. They were all fear and panic. I'm sure that mine only showed ferocity. I did not claw her. I held her and smelled her and waited for her to cease her struggling. I had her well within my grasp. She didn't have a chance. She was going nowhere. I was only waiting for her to realize it. I licked her face. She probably thought it a cruel prelude. But it was a show of my affection.

She calmed. She stopped her struggle. What I really wanted was to take her to some foreign land. Somewhere where the others around wouldn't see it so strange; we could cohabit. We could mate. Our offspring could have my strength and her grace. Surely they would be the most beautiful and revered beings on the planet. I held her close and felt the beating of her quickened heart in her beautiful breast. I smelled her, caressed her, confounded her. I slowly wrapped my jaws around her throat. I breathed in as deep as I ever had. As the air left my lungs, I tightened my jaws around her. My long, razor sharp teeth sunk into her flesh with the precision I have always relied on. Her blood filled my mouth and urged my actions onward. Welcome to your end, my darling; welcome to your death, my love.

Hers' was neither a slow, nor a prolonged death. I simply held her body near to mine. My paws caressed her and I enjoyed the thought of our hearts beating in unison, but my heart rate couldn't keep up with hers'. Her blood filled and overflowed my jaws and the light and life seeped out of her eyes and she –after some time– was gone. I feasted slowly upon her breast and body for three days. For three days I basked in what was remaining of the perfume of her body. Her meat was sweat and tender. I took her just right and left a very palatable corpse. For those three days, I laid in the sun and slowly made her body disappear. I jaunted to and from the lake to quench my thirst. I laid, semi-surprised, for all this time, unchallenged and unbothered. She was enough meal for me and the other herbivores knew it. So they weren't too shy about visiting the lake for thirst and cleanliness. Her family even came back for the peaceful beach the lake provided. They looked at me in horror. But I am what I am. I saw her; I chased her; I killed her and claimed her corpse. Birds didn't bother me and no other predator challenged me. It was as if the other predators knew what she had become to me and how far I travelled for her. There was nothing left to do with my love for her, but to feast on her. I enjoyed her feast with sensual, almost sexual bliss. My hunger and my habit did not allow a lamentation. That came later.

My jog home was nothing like my chase. I said farewell to the forest. My salute was in no way returned. Only the slow muting of the sounds, the fading colors and the dying perfumes of the forest. I wasn't urged on by my hunger and desire, but ushered home by comfort and familiarity. The taste of her flesh still hung in my mouth. My fur was stained with her blood. The memory of her, in every stage of our encounter was still at the forefront of my mind. When I left, there was nothing left of her but scraps for the birds and the dogs. I chased her farther than I'd ever chased anything. As far as I am concerned, that forest was at the end of the Earth, much farther than I'd ever travelled in my entire life. She was the most enticing creature I'd ever seen, and I have seen many gazelles in my lifetime, many beautiful creatures out here on the plains. She was my greatest challenge to date and I met her with all that characterizes my species. I was true to myself and hold no regret in my heart. There was never any chance of anything more than what I received. I carried my bulging stomach home. I would carry her in my mind for all the remaining days of my life. She surely will slip from forefront to background, but she will always be there … the great chase of my life; the creature that coaxed me out of my comfortable kingdom and into the forest. Call it the forest of my desire.

Chapter 28

I did call it, The Forest of My Desire, by George Wordworthy. And that is how it appeared in print, and it was printed in more than one publication, but that all comes later. My stay in Suley's house in the Lower East Side was a comfort and I did feel like a king while I was there. I didn't have to clean anything. I didn't have to cook anything. I was waited on and attended to as Suleyman himself was. I had never known such luxury. I slept and wrote in a spare room. Down the hall was Suley and Hondai, Erman, Eiden. They each had their rooms with solid wooden doors. The halls were long and wide. There was space for us all.

We lived like a family, like siblings in a home devoid of parents. But we were not destructive adolescents or needy children. We simply were. We ate together each morning. Erman was the administrator of their business. He looked over the books. He dealt with the management of the Lounge. He made sure everything ran smoothly while Suley selected the entertainment and invited the guests. He walked through The Lounge once each night to grace his guests. Otherwise, it was uncertain if he spent very much time attending the nightly festivities. Eiden watched the door and was the security. He was a capable and confident man.

The first few days I was there, I didn't write a thing. There was a desk and chair for me in my room, and a typewriter and a tall stack of white pages. I sat at it after breakfast the first morning I was there. I sat there and loaded a page into the typewriter, but I didn't strike a key and the page remained blank. I sat in the room and felt the space. I looked at the sparse decorations. It was an unused room, uninhabited until my arrival. I felt the space. I looked out the window, the buildings across the slim street. I felt glad to be there, but I wasn't ready to write. I searched all three levels of their home. Three dens, five bathrooms, two kitchens, two dining rooms. Rugs hung on walls. Candles stood in silver candlesticks. There were paintings; some looked like they must have been traditional Turkish paintings, others were modern era paintings and post modern.

They had two servants, both older women who did not speak much. They came every morning to make breakfast and left every night after dinner. They cooked and they cleaned. They made each of our beds while we ate. They filled our glasses and our plates. They washed and pressed our clothes. I didn't know how to treat them or what to say to them. I didn't even know if they spoke English; they never spoke. I simply thanked them when they served me, and when I saw them in passing in the halls. It was an altogether alien experience.

I didn't stay cooped up there. I found my musician friends and listened to them play and laughed with them when they were finished. I met up with Noah once while I was there and he was happy to hear that I was back to writing. I saw Keisha often. She had an intense effect on me. I wondered sometimes how our love would last. The intensity was so high. I feared that it was unsustainable. I buried these fears. We went to museums. We danced at clubs. We watched movies and plays and ate together. There were plenty of nights when she worked and I left her alone with her friends.

It had been so exciting to meet her for the first time, to wonder when and if I might see her again, to chase her. Then I spent a lot of time impressing her with my money and good taste. But we were getting to a point where I wasn't sure what to do. We were getting familiar. We were telling each other our secrets. We were illuminating the paths of our lives and the hardships we'd experienced along the way. The excitement was starting to fade. That isn't to say that I didn't still feel the magnetism between us. That was strong. I looked into her eyes and felt the power of the cosmos; we were in love. But I had no experience with that sort of thing. I knew how to make love, the physical act of love and we spent hours sweating in each other's arms. I knew how to talk and make her laugh and how to enjoy her stories and her company. But I didn't know what to do about our growing familiarity. I didn't know what to think of it, or how to cope with it because as that familiarity grew, the narcotic effects of our union diminished.

The story started to come to me. Inspiration drew me to the room that Suley leant me. I kept a hot cup of tea nearby. I didn't know what I was writing at first so I just started filling pages. Most of it was nonsense. Most of what I was writing, I never shared with anyone and those pages ended up in the waste bin. But my fingers were becoming familiar with the keys of the typewriter, and that familiarity was something that brought me comfort. I went through many false starts before I found the setting of Africa. I wanted to see pictures and do research, but there was no computer in Suleyman's home. That I had a hard time understanding. They seemed to pay no mind to the technological developments of the time. They didn't even have cell phones. It was mind boggling to me.

I searched the books in Suley's vast library for information. I found pictures in local museums. I felt out the essence of what African culture might be through exhibits around town, wood carvings and dung sculptures, paintings made by visiting Europeans, pictures from photographers all around the world; they all went to Africa for inspiration. I felt a jealousy in my heart having never been there myself. But I had never really been much of anywhere. New York City was my one big exploration, my first.

The beginning of the story came to me in a dream after days of exploration in books and at museums. I skipped breakfast that morning and spent hours on my first paragraph. There are so many angles to tell a story from, so many contrasts to consider. I didn't know the plot or the characters. I only knew the setting. I dreamt of the animals. I dreamt of being a lion. The dream itself was fleeting. I tried to capture the feeling. I nurtured the story. I let it grow. I typed. Then I revised. I edited the pages with a pen. I retyped. I re-edited. I spent a month on this little story. A whole month working out the plot, the narrations, the characterization, the details, the dialogue and then the realization that there could be none. There was so much more detail I wanted to put in place. I wanted to include everything that I'd learned about Africa, about the deserts and the jungles and the plains, but all those details only confused the emotion of the story. I was disappointed with the size of the story when I knew I was done with it. I knew I was done with it and there was nothing more to add or to take away. It was a spartan seven pages. I had been given so much and all I had created in return was this measly story. It was short and I could not make it any longer, but I was happy with it.

Chapter 29

I wasn't sure how I felt about the integrity of the story. I wasn't sure that it was all that good. But I didn't know if I could do any better. So I didn't say anything to Suley about it for a couple of days and he didn't ask. We ate together and talked small. Their business was improving by leaps and bounds and it was very successful in the first place. His parties were largely by invitation only and he was having a hard time keeping his guest list to a comfortable capacity. He grinned. Erman boasted boisterously. Eiden fretted as security was getting tougher to manage. It was hard for him to turn away the powerful people who more eagerly stopped by without invitation.

As I stayed silent about my completed story, I revisited the museums, galleries, and bookstores that so inspired and leant information to me of the cultures and sights of Africa. I reread my story over and over again, looking for imperfections to improve and analyzing for integrity. It was hard for me. I hadn't shown anything I'd written to anyone since college and as a student – I was more hopeful than talented. My grades were good, but nothing to get crazy about. I questioned myself and my abilities. I didn't want to disappoint Suleyman who had shown a very calm confidence in me. He looked at me and saw an artist, a writer. There was no question of it in his mind. When I looked in the mirror, I only saw my face as I shaved off the stubble. It's an alright face. I looked into my own eyes. I saw doubt and hope simultaneously. I didn't know if I saw any kind of great talent.

When I couldn't read my story any longer, when the words on the page only melded into blotches and no sense of its meaning or lyricism signaled to me, I knew it was time. I had detached my emotions from it. If he didn't think it was worth anything, it wouldn't break me. If he thought it was total shit, it wouldn't knock me down. If he loved it and admired me for it, it wouldn't swell my head. I started thinking when a good time to show it to him would be. When would he be most receptive? I didn't know. So I just told him about it over breakfast one morning. My quiet announcement hushed the table. Their eyes landed on me. I didn't know what to think of this. It was as if I suddenly had a power and that power was to shut up my company and draw their attention to myself.

Suley wiped his mouth clean and swallowed and looked at me. Before I'd spoken, I didn't think I was about to interrupt anything, but after the words passed my lips and I saw the effect, I wondered if I should have chosen another moment. You're finished, Suley asked and he seemed surprised, as if he'd assumed it would have taken longer. It's just a short story, I said. What's it about, man, Erman projected his businessman mentality as the take charge extrovert that he is. I stumbled on his question. I was somehow unprepared to speak on the subject. I'd simply assumed that Suley would read it and judge me. I thought momentarily on the question. I said: it's a love story. A love story, Eiden asked. It's a hunting tale, I said. A hunting tale, Suley grinned. A love story and a hunting tale, Erman asked. Yes, I said; it's animalistic. Does that mean it's pornographic, Erman chided and Eiden laughed with him. Hondai cast a harsh glance at them for their indiscretion. Who is in love, she asked. A lion, I answered. Is there a hunter, Hondai asked. The lion is the hunter, I said; he's also the narrator. Does it have a happy ending, she asked. I don't know if it's happy, I said, but it ends. All great things do, Suley said and I wasn't sure how to take it. Well, let's see it, he said.

I left the breakfast table and ran up the stairs to my room and took the pages that I'd left next to the typewriter. I handed him the pages and told him it was my only copy. I will take care with it, he said. Hondai smiled peacefully at him and touched his hand. This was something that she loved in him, his ability to be delicate and sensitive. I will read it later, he said. And there was a silence that came to the table and it made me uncomfortable. I felt like I'd ruined the usually clamorously conversational ambiance of our morning gathering. I felt it was my duty to change the conversation to something more palatable to the company. So I asked who highlighted this night's guest list. The tension between my companions subsided and conversation resumed along the usual comfortable lines of parties and guests and the minutia that makes each night at The Turkish Lounge a success.

Chapter 30

Days went by and we saw each other, but Suley said nothing of my story. After a few days, he asked me if I was ready to get back to work; customers were asking for me. My absence had been noticed; the wealthy junkies missed me. I don't know why. I never really stayed that long. Our conversations were always short and sparse. But they were asking for me all the same. It was still too cold and icy for the Vespa. I found myself back in the Heights, dressing myself as if I were going to work on Wall Street. And in a way I was. There was a new client down there, in a townhouse at the Southern most tip of Manhattan. She had large bay windows overlooking the Atlantic, with a clear view of the Statue of Liberty. She told me her husband ran a small, sophisticated investment group in the heart of Wall Street. She said he worked often and often worked late. I gave her a few grams of various heroin. She was a woman who liked variety, she said in a seductive way and she was a beautiful woman. She asked me to stay with her. She invited me to join her. She wanted me to shoot up with her. I contemplated it. One of the reasons I was hired is because I was unafraid to dive into the deep end of absurd behaviors. But in my mind, it was one thing to try something like heroin; it was another thing to make a habit of it. I knew it was a habit that I didn't want. I'd never shot up with a client before and I didn't want this to be a first of many times. I was torn on the subject, but not having any other appointments for several hours, I told her that I would keep her company.

I asked her what her interests were, but she wasn't interested in discussing them. I asked her more about her husband and if they had children. She wasn't interested in talking about that either. I didn't know what to say. I got up to leave, but she didn't want that either. She asked me to shoot it into her, to assist her in her self medication, to act as her nurse for a moment. She said she'd tip me well for it. I used a silk tie from a robe that she had out and used it as a tourniquet. I readied a spoon and mixed the water and powder. I tapped her arm. Her veins were far from the surface. I'd never done this for anyone before and I didn't want to make a pin cushion out of her arm. As I searched for a vein, she became irritated with me. Just shove it in, she exasperated. A moment later, I found a vein and plunged the needle in. I drew out some of the sanguine within her. There was something mesmerizing about watching the blood mix with the dark liquid of the heroin solution. I pushed steadily on the plunger and watched her face change from irritation to ecstasy; it was like turning a switch. She was no longer some irritable housewife, unsatisfied by all the adornments and riches provided her. She was consumed by a childish ecstasy. She laid back on her sofa and caressed her own cheek and neck. She dipped a hand into her blouse and caressed a breast. She grabbed my hand and pulled it toward her, but I stopped her. I said I couldn't. I had a girlfriend. I was in love. She laughed at me and made fun of me; the drug dealer has a girlfriend, she exclaimed as if someone else were there to hear her and join in, in mocking me, but no one else was there. I felt terrible, as if I'd done something wrong, as if I'd betrayed Keisha. I told her I had to leave. She demanded that I stay; this was a woman used to getting what she wanted, so used to it that it was absurd to her that I should deny her authority. I couldn't stay and I knew it; but the last thing I needed was her badmouthing me to Suley.

I left without a tip. I felt degraded and ashamed. I asked Mohammed to take me straight and quickly to The Turkish Lounge. I was obviously upset and he asked what it was. I couldn't bring myself to get into with him. He shrugged and drove. I was anxious to get to Suley's ear. I needed him to hear direct from me and in person what happened. The woman was noticeably upset with me when I left and God only knows what she might say to Suley about me. I didn't trust her. I didn't understand such a woman, a married woman. I understand that the rich act in certain ways. I've read a lot of books and watched movies. Who knows why she married or what she assumed or knew he did behind her back, but I wasn't about to be a part of some revenge plot and I didn't want her spreading rumors, especially none that would get back to Keisha.

I found Suley and he was busy and didn't want to be interrupted, but I begged for a moment of his time. I got it. I told him what happened. He didn't laugh at me. He apologized. I was getting sick of this job, I told him. It was all fun and mischief when I started and people hardly gave me the time of day, just money. But this, this is bullshit. He talked to calm me down. I didn't want to disappoint him or seem ungrateful for all he'd done, but things were getting out of hand. It wasn't a job that was going to lead anywhere and I couldn't go on delivering drugs for him. My rose colored glasses were slipping off my face and I was starting to really realize what I was doing. His brow furrowed and he sighed. I don't think he knew what to say to me. People like you, George. I don't want to see you go. It's hard to find someone to trust to take care of this kind of sensitive business. The money is good for you, he said. She didn't tip me, I said. Forget her, he said. She's done. I'll take care of her. You don't have to go there anymore. Try to avoid these situations in the future, he told me. He didn't want this kind of thing any more than I did. He couldn't allow any friction between he and his customers. It was not only bad for business, but bad for his own safety and security. Do you have any other deliveries today, he asked. I did. Finish off your day and start tomorrow anew, he said. Put this incident in the back of your mind, he said; forget it.

On my next delivery, I remembered what he said. I didn't stray far from the doorway and didn't open my mouth except to utter the price. My smile was fleeting. I was not going to let anything like it happen again. By the end of the day I was tired. I was really tired. A day of deliveries hadn't ever run me down so much. I was really stressed and run down and the worst part of it was that that woman had gotten to me. The worst part of it was the nagging desire within me. She was an attractive woman. Physically she was attractive. Otherwise, not so much. But I did take some delight in watching her touch herself and it made me feel guilty.

The last delivery of the day came. It was to a guy my own age. He was pleasant and easy going and he asked me in. He told me I looked stressed. He handed over a wad of bills and took his dope. He sat down and kept talking as he mixed it and shot up. A doggish smile plastered his face. So what are you really, he asked as he leaned back into a comfortable chair, his leg hanging over an arm of. He lit a cigarette. What, I asked. What are you … really? Come on, let it out, he said. This isn't your great aspiration. You're not a Turk, I can tell. Suley picked you up here in this city, but you're from somewhere else, he said. How can you tell, I asked. He tossed me a cigarette. I was still near the door. He tossed me a book of matches.

I've lived in this town all my life, he said. I can tell the Manhattanites from the out-of-towners. You're a small towner, he said. You're in way over your head. Suleyman is using you up. You're his buffer from authority. You're the fall guy, he laughed. My face changed and he sympathized. Hey man, it's not like you're unaware of what you're doing. You just don't understand the severity of your actions. But that's not what's bothering you, he said. No, something else is on your mind. I'm psychic, you know, he said. That's how I know all this. I get it from my father. He was one of Wall Street's best. He made a million by the time he was twenty. It's great. He really pissed people off. He was a first generation here. He grew up in a firetrap apartment in Greenpoint, the son of Polish immigrants. He worked for them at the butcher shop my grandfather owned. The place was going under the year my dad turned twenty and my grandfather was beside himself. He gave his son the last thousand dollars that he had and told him to go to the market and buy something with it. He knew my dad. He was good at math and always seemed to know what was going to happen before it did. Go prove your gift, is what he said to my father. Dad took the money down to Wall Street and that was the end of it. Granddad lived off of dividends for the rest of his life, but they brought the butcher shop back to life first. Dad never looked back. I heard that story a thousand times. I even worked on Wall Street for a year after college. Too fucking crazy for me. I just day trade from home now. Piece of cake.

My name is Jarek, he said and held out his hand for me to shake. Jarek Podgurski, he said. I smiled faintly but didn't take a step away from the door. Oh hey, man, he said, I'm no fag. Come in. Sit down, unless you're busy. If you have to go, I don't want to keep you. You're having a rough time, he said. I sighed. I didn't think I was having a rough time, I said. I thought I was getting a free ride. Free rides are deceptive, he said. Ask the prostitute or the day trader. Ask anyone, he said. Life is deceptive, he said. You think it's gotten easy. You lay back and bask in it. The universe has lined up for you. Your life isn't going to be the hell that so many endure, right, he said. And then something happens. What happened, he said. The cops on to you? That question made me nervous. He claims to be a psychic. Be careful, he said. Your game is dangerous.

You seem like a smart guy to me, I told him; what are you doing this shit for? That's what you say to your customers, he asked. What would Suley think of it? I looked him in the eye. I told him that I didn't worry that he'd rat me out to Suley. I didn't care anymore. There was too much bullshit starting with this job. Customers were getting friendly and that was seemingly a dangerous thing in itself. For instance I said, and then I went on to tell him the earlier events of my day. He expressed his jealousy. It's been too long since I've had a woman, he said, let alone some pent up housewife hotty. He asked me for her number, her address. I didn't feel comfortable giving it to him. I told him, you don't want to deal with that shit. That is exactly the kind of shit I would love to deal with, he said. Instead I'm stuck here all the time. Can't leave the fucking computer. The whores I have come by, they gave me herpes, he said. Now all I have for sexual satisfaction is heroin. Heroin and whores. But I don't really like the hookers anymore.

I couldn't believe that he was serious about all that. He assured me that he was. He reminded me that it's a hard and dark road that leads to heroin. And then, somehow, he convinced me to shoot up with him. He had a pile of clean, hermetically sealed needles. The last thing I remember thinking was, what the hell is wrong with me. I don't know if it was a question and I didn't answer it. I just dove in once more. Into the darkening abyss, into my cold, dark inner world. I surfed at Barracuda level and found a pleasure in drowning.

I don't know what it was that really got to me that day. I don't know what it was that sent me down to that level, into that darkness. But I laughed. Jarek laughed and he screamed and I screamed. I sprawled out on his couch. He sat in his chair. He shot himself up again and he mumbled to himself. I laughed and let my eyes roll back and felt the pleasure of nothingness. My eyes rolled back down again and I stared at my feet and just stared at them, at those shoes. I just stared and stared. Nothing came into my mind until I felt sick. Jarek lit a joint and passed it to me. He turned on some video games and we played seek and destroy missions on his giant flat screen. Hours slipped away.

Some time in the late hours of the night, I stepped out onto a sidewalk and puked and coughed. Mohammad wasn't outside waiting like I thought he would be. All for the best. I'd rather Suley didn't find out that I spent hours with a customer shooting up and slacking off. One of the things I think he liked about me was that I didn't indulge. I didn't openly judge and I wasn't a junkie myself. I crossed a line tonight. I crossed it and I didn't care. I didn't care and I caught a cab home. I felt sick and disgusting the whole ride. I gave the cabby too much money. I didn't care. I usually got too much money. I was a profiteer of death and self destruction. But I'm not a whore. I'm not and I will not be. That is not why I came here. I didn't come here to die either. I didn't come here to turn into fucking junkie. I did not.

I laid shaking and awake for hours in my bed. I drank water by the gallon and puked it up minutes later. My skin burned and I was freezing. My guts twisted and my eyes were hot. I could not find any comfort anywhere. I wanted to escape my body. It had become a torturous, riotous prison. All I felt was suffering and pain.

This was the pleasure that I was bringing people. This ... this! My illusions were fading. I was a harbinger of torture and pain; I was bringing the punishment of the ages. I was a fucking asshole. But I couldn't stop. It wasn't the drugs I was addicted to. It was the false sense of security. It was the money, the lifestyle, the lack of effort. By the time day broke, it was easy and true to say that I hated myself.

Chapter 31

I met with Suley in his office in The Turkish
Lounge. He sat behind the desk very business like.
He called me in for this meeting. It was too
formal. I felt uncomfortable. It felt wrong. I'd
assumed that he'd digested the recent incidences
between me and his customers and I thought that
this was the end of our business relationship. I
was beyond the point of caring about the job itself.
It was wearing on me and I would have welcomed
a reasonable excuse to let it go. To be fired from it
was just as well. It isn't like I'd be able to use it on
a resume. But the thought that these
transgressions would dissolve our friendship was
a frightening thought. I had enough money piled
under my bed that not having an income for a few
months was no longer something that made me
nervous. Thank you very much, Suley. And it
was that very admission of his grandiose help that
chilled my blood to think that I may have upset
him enough to entice him to dissolve our
friendship. In short, I was afraid. No longer afraid

for my own wellbeing, but afraid that I'd hurt the very person who never neglected to help me. He helped me and I had nothing really to offer him. Jarek believes that Suley was using me as a way to buffer him from the authorities, but I thought that my place in Suley's association was more dangerous for him than it was for me. He had much more to lose.

Suley placed his hands on his desk near stacks of paper work. He had a rotary phone. You look nervous, George, he told me. Do I, I asked. I hated feeling that I am transparent. He grinned and I didn't know what to think. There's no need to be, he said. You don't know why I asked you in? There weren't any deliveries at the moment. It was otherwise a seeming day off which I didn't have that often. There's nothing to worry about, George ... is your conscious getting to you, he asked. I shrugged. I didn't know where any of this was going and I didn't want to expose myself. It's a hard job in some respects, he said; I understand that this whole business can mess with a person's conscience. I myself have had those moments. It only means that you are human and a decent human at that, George. You are only giving them what they want. If it wasn't us, it would be someone else. At least I can guarantee the purity of our product. Overdoses of our customers are rare. You know, George, I will never blame you if you want to quit. I will never hold it against you if you feel that it's not something you want to be involved in. Just remember that we are friends, he said.

So, you're not upset with me then, I asked him. Why should I be upset with you, George? You do the job well; you're always presentable and polite. Many of our customers treasure your presence. You have that American thing ... you come off as puritanical and quaint. It comforts the natural fears that people in our association often have. You know, I hadn't considered the service that you are enabling us to provide until you came to me. I couldn't feel comfortable sending out Eiden or Erman. They don't have the time and they are too close to the business, but you, you are doing a great job, George and I'm sorry about your encounter with Mrs. Goff the other day. I looked at him with a lack of comprehension. Oh, come on, George, she was the woman down on Wall Street, he said. She tried to seduce you. You know, he laughed, most men in your position would have climbed all over her. She's an attractive woman. But you, he smiled. You, George, are in a relationship and you know that she is married. The thought of sleeping with her disturbed you, he laughed. That is so quaint and puritanical. This is what we all like about you.

So you're not upset with me, I asked. No, George, Suley said. Why did you think that? Well, why did you want to see me? Here? So formally in your office? I feel like I've been called to the principal's office. He laughed, what like primary school, he asked. Yeah, I replied. Yeah, he parroted back to me. It's a very busy time for us now, George. I have been on the phone all morning. Honestly, it's been such a headache today … I wanted to see you, get some down time. Besides, he said, I have good news for you. News, I asked. Did you forget already, he asked. The Forest of My Desire, George – your short story. You worked for six weeks on that little story. I wonder about you sometimes. Have you forgotten about it, he asked. No, I said, I just … I don't know. What about it, I asked. George, you know I am very well connected here among many other places, but I could never twist the arm of an editor to publish something that didn't meet the standard of their publication. You called me in to tell me that the story I haven't been thinking about isn't getting published, I asked him. I felt confused. I felt like he was messing with me. I felt like everybody was messing with me. What was going on?

Suley started to describe to me the way it went down. He invited to The Lounge a friend of his from New York Reader Magazine. He's one of the head editors of the magazine and Suley started talking to him about me and my story. But what really surprised me was that this guy had already heard of me. I guess that I'd been introduced to enough people as the young writer George Wordworthy that this guy had remembered my name. God knows what kind of rumors had been attached to my name, but they couldn't have been too bad because the guy was interested in reading my story for the simple reason of matching up my work with my name. I found that alone to be interesting and flattering. So Suley gives him the only copy of the story and leaves it at that. A few weeks later he calls Suley up on the phone and he's really excited. He said he'd been wondering what this new writer was up to. He said that he'd googled me and found nothing about any writer with my name and was starting to think that I was a fictional character that some of his friends and associates had made up. He thought that they'd been messing with him.

First thing, he accused Suley of being the young writer, writing under the pseudonym George Wordworthy, which made Suley ecstatic. And Suley's denials only made the editor's suspicions seem more valid to him. Suley would not give in and tell the editor the lie that he most dearly wanted to hear. He wouldn't admit that he was me. Instead he pressed the editor to get to the point of the telephone conversation. The rest of this retelling is just me gloating. It's all flattery. It was embarrassing for me to listen to, even if it did inflate my ego and accelerate my imagination. I started seeing myself as I was in my early writer fantasies and before that realization could scare me back into reality, I basked in the stunning sunlight and wonder of a dream fulfilled.

I left Suley's office on a cloud and as I walked out onto the street, I pulled out my phone. I called my folks back in PA. Dad gave me the attaboy, but Mom was all – oh, I knew it and then her imagination of my writer fantasies were ignited and we basked together in my possible future and when we hung up I was left with a boyhood feeling of accomplishment and an emotional reuniting with my mother which in an embarrassing way was a good feeling. I called Gram out in Jersey and we scheduled lunch together for the following Sunday.

The person I was most excited to tell was one of the last people I told. Keisha met me again at Le Petite Café. We had coffee and shared a piece of tiramisu. They have the best tiramisu in town. I told her my good news and her face lit up. All her beauty reached out to me. Her featured features: eyes, lips, the glow of her face, the cool touch of her long fingers, the wisps of hair that constantly fall from behind her ear to veil her face only to be pushed back behind her ear again, her long neck and slim shoulders and the energy that she cast my way that lifted me always to my higher self. Ours was a quiet celebration in our little coffee shop. We stayed there together for hours talking small and enjoying each other and I enjoyed that she enjoyed my company as much as I enjoyed enjoying hers.

Chapter 32

Something was brewing around The
Turkish Lounge. Suley and Erman were all
secretive energy abounding. They were all electric,
but their lips were sealed. Something was going
on; something was being masterminded. I didn't
know what it was or how I was going to be
affected, but it didn't seem like anything devious
and there was no fear surrounding it. I was still
floating in the ethers about the publication of my
short story. After it was published in New York
Reader Magazine, it was printed in small
publications around the country. Everyone was
congratulating me. I was like a favored pet all of a
sudden and came to know the satisfaction of being
appreciated for a talent. My metaphorical tail was
wagging with unflagging consistency. It was a
good feeling, the feeling of accomplishment. And
many were starting to ask me what I was going to
write next. I was starting to think about what *my*
New York City story was going to be.

The mystery of my Turkish friends was starting to unravel as clues came to me from every angle. My first clue was that it was going to have something to do with the Mandarin Hotel. Then I found that Alice and Sam would be in some ways involved. Then Keisha mentioned something about Suley and Erman being up to something 'exciting'. Kidd and Jarvis were to be involved and so were Charles and Joe. As the weeks wore on, my intrigue grew.

Suddenly all the musicians in our circle were buzzing with questions, excitement and rumors. I brought my suspicions to Noah and he laughed. You guys are always up to no good; it's hard to tell what's going on, he said. We were back at Croxley's. It was Friday. Wings are free as long as you buy a beer at Croxley's on Fridays. That's the main reason that we went. They were good fat wings and the beer was cold and bubbling out of the tap and Noah was good company, consistently.

The next time Keisha and I were together, we were all curiosity and speculation. We were whispers and kisses and soft fingers gliding on warm skin. She was giggles and I was laughter and it was all just fun and speculation. But she gave me the biggest clue that I would receive. She was being paid by Suley to be at the Mandarin Hotel and ready to perform a fortnight from our private moment in time. Then later that night we found out that Sam and Alice and Joe and Charles were also booked by Suley for that night. Then a few days later we were with Jarvis and Kidd and they were booked by Suley as well. The list of musicians was growing.

The show space at the Mandarin is no small venue. Knowing Suley, he wouldn't shell out the money for such a space unless he was confident he would fill it. And then, as I bounced around town delivering the precious poisons I was paid to deliver, I found that each and every one of those customers was brimming with excitement about the event scheduled to take place at the Mandarin Hotel. None of them knew much about the night's festivities, but they all had a definite faith in Suley and Erman to throw a great party.

Then one afternoon Suley gave me a call. He wanted me to meet him at the Mandarin Hotel in an hour. It was all to be revealed. When I arrived at the hotel, I discovered what all the secrecy was about and I was being involved in the crux of the secret. Eiden needed help setting up the recording equipment. It was an extensive array of electronics and microphones. I didn't know too much about setting up this sort of thing, but I followed Eiden's instruction and in the end I did a good job.

It was Suley's greatest gamble to date. Not only was he going to record the great wealth of New York City's underground and unrecorded Jazz musicians, he was branding his own label. He was a little on edge. He knew the myriad ways a night like this could pan out. Most of all he was anxious about the musicians themselves showing up and showing up on time. After that, he was hoping that they wouldn't mind being recorded. He hadn't told them that that was his plan. It was all a sneak attack on his part and I told him that I thought that was a little devious. He told me he couldn't imagine any other way that he could realistically bring it all together. He wasn't even sure that he would tell them before the event was over and he made me swear that I wouldn't tell any of them. I thought hard on the idea. He was asking me to deceive my friends. Though I did think it was a good idea and he swore to me that it would benefit them as much as it would him. All the same, there were real reasons why some of them wouldn't want to be recorded. In the end I promised not to tell my friends. But when he reminded me that this included Keisha, I started to have second thoughts and feel guilty about it. I really didn't think that this opportunity was one that she would pass up. I didn't think that if she knew she'd be upset at all, but she might be upset with me for keeping such a secret from her and she would inevitably find out that I helped in the setup of the equipment and thus find out that I did know beforehand. There was only one logical thing for me to do in this situation. I lied. I lied to my friend and benefactor. I lied to Suleyman, straight to his face, and promised that I wouldn't tell Keisha a thing. But when she arrived, I took her back stage and made her promise she wouldn't tell anyone, no matter how ridiculous and silly a thing it seemed to keep secret. I spilled my guts to her. I spilled them and her first reaction was elation that she was being recorded. Her second reaction was negative; it was directed at Suley's deception. She expressed concern that Suley was planning to steal the music and not give her or any of them anything for it. Such things have happened between artists and producers in the past and she said that she would rather go on living relatively unrecognized than to have someone outrightly steal her music and sell it without her obtaining anything from it. That is when I reminded her of my story and its publication. I received full credit and royalties for those publications. Suley was glad to help and glad to have another talent in his entourage. Suley had shitloads of money. He was far more interested in the prestige of having talent at his disposal and in his circle than profiting financially.

Keisha accepted what I believed Suley's intentions to be, but that didn't stop her from confronting him. She told him she wouldn't perform without a contract. She was direct and stern and unwavering. And she also told him that she was telling the rest of them. It should be for each artist to decide when and where and for how much they are willing to be recorded and distributed. Suley found himself in a hard position. He looked at me with hard eyes and I at him with apologetic eyes, but in the end we both knew that it was he who put himself in this situation, not me. Suley put Erman in a panic to have all the paperwork written. Contracts for all of them. Royalties and rights. Everyone got exactly the same. Suley wasn't favoring anyone, which upset Jarvis and Powell. Everyone else accepted that this is where their roads had lead them. It was one contract that Erman had drawn up. It was only the names that changed. Everyone accepted that Suley was giving them a fair shake, everyone but Jarvis and Powell. They were the last to sign. They waited until they knew for a fact that the show would go on without them if they so chose. Their hesitation didn't have too much to do with their percentage which was high, it was the lack of preferential treatment that irked them.

Backstage, it was me and my girl and all my musician friends. It was celebratory. It was excitement and elation. It was real enthusiasm. A jittery, jarring feeling swept between them. Nerves were fraying and well displayed. I'd never seen any of them like this before a show and by this time I'd been to more shows with them than I could count on all my fingers and toes.

The only performer who wasn't openly excited and on edge was Bud Powell. He didn't talk. He didn't move. He sat in a straight-back chair. His face betrayed no emotions. His was either a portrait of calm, or he was the most nervous of all of them. Keisha looked out from behind the vast curtain and feasted her eyes upon the amassing crowd. I joined her. There were a lot of people; it was looking like the large hall was going to fill to capacity. She confessed to me that she'd never played a show this large. Except for Jarvis Wrightly and Powell, I don't think any of them ever had.

Her hands were shaking and her skin was pale. I told her to take a deep breath … that this was going to be a great moment in her life. I told her that this was the beginning of her success and that everything that came after it would be a reflection of this night. I told her that she was going to be wonderful. I told her that she was wonderful. I told her that I loved her, that I was in love with her. I kissed her and I held her. She shook for a moment in my arms and she wept. I held her tight until she shook no more. Her tear moistened lips touched mine and she held my face and kissed me and kissed me gently, then passionately, then softly.

Sam and Alice, in the grips of their own moment, came to peek out into the open room to spy the crowd as well. Every hope and dream they had ever had was engendered in this gathering; this event was the spark they had all been avoiding for fear of failure and defeat. It was upon them and inescapable. They could do only one thing and that was to put on the best show that their combined talent could produce. This was their night and all their friends were there to be a part of it.

Erman stepped backstage and Suleyman stepped on to the stage. They spoke nearly simultaneously and I didn't know where to throw my attention. Suley spoke calmly and excitedly into the center stage microphone while Erman was limited to the power of his own voice. Suley's audience were the thousand plus people in attendance. Erman's audience was the dozen or so performers to go on. Suley spoke of the momentous event that he was proud to present. Erman spoke more in a rallying battle cry to give confidence and verve to the performers. Both were uplifting and evocative. Both assumed their roll with clarity and precision. Both Suley and Erman delivered their speeches better than most politicians I've seen on television broadcasts. Suley received for his efforts a thunderous round of applause that foretold the praise that these musicians would receive. Erman garnered an appreciative and contemplative uplifting of spirit and quieting of nerves. They were each orators of perfect design for their places in this moment.

Erman explained that their first performance, as would the final performance, be a group performance. No other instruction was given. There was no sheet music, which would have been an insult to most if not all of these musicians. This is Jazz we're talking about. Jazz is musical improvisation; its fever and flight are what make the genre. The energy produced in the last hour backstage awaiting these first moments was all the motivation and instruction these musicians needed to perform, but knowing this group, that stage was going to become a battleground.

They brandished their instruments like Marines brandishing their weapons. Their eyes cast upon each other. Each making their plan of attack. They could have tried to plan an orchestration, but the curtains were parting; it would have to be figured out openly on the stage. A sudden bolt of anxiety struck my stomach as I skulked into the background and my musician friends walked to the forefront of the stage.

I don't know how they did it. There were no outward arguments or discussions, as if they were functioning telepathically; they were functioning organically, as one mechanism. They were a tribute to fate, to destiny; they proved to me that these forces exist because their improvised performance was flawless.

Applause rained down upon them when the curtains parted. Some of my friends bowed. Some stood stoic and absorbed this opening praise. They each assumed their posture. They each were ready to play. Joe sat at the drums; he was easily the least contained of all and he was ready to explode with volume through those drums. It was Jarvis Wrightly who broke through the static of silence, a king's call. Joe came in with a marching beat on snare and two toms; it was as if he had six arms. Sam broke in and Kidd followed suit. Charles and a few others, whom I did not know, followed suit. Keisha was strumming along on her guitar; it was strange for her to mix in with all these instruments, being a solo artist. Powell sat at the grand piano with his arms crossed, refusing to play until the moment was his, and when it was, he proved his abilities.

Alice hung back with me until the time was ripe and when it was, she and Keisha shared the center stage microphone and their voices merged to produce such music of which I have never heard. It was as if two angels had joined forces to call upon the ears of God. This entire group of musicians dazzled the audience, myself, Erman, Eiden, Suleyman, and I believe they wowed themselves as well. The orchestra was turbulent; it fell from grace to cacophony and into harmony and then swung with intense rhythm.

The curtains fell and applause roared. The audience was an amazing group themselves, some of the most talented and powerful people associated with New York City. There were tables set up café style, a bevy of bars, an army of servers, and room to dance. Erman acted as general of the musicians. And when the curtains fell he was on the stage in the midst of mayhem without concern of his own wellbeing. Kidd was the first to take the stage, the opening act and he could recruit whomever he liked out of who was willing. He took Joe and Charles. Joe was an electric maniac ready for a long, hard night. Charles took a deep breath and steadied himself. Erman ushered the rest back stage and Keisha back into my arms. I doled out praise and confidence to her; it was my job and my pleasure to be at her side this night. She was going to perform her role in this evening elegantly and I was going to comfort her in exactly the ways she needed.

Kidd opened with what was probably the best performance he had ever given, proving once and for all that he belonged in the company he kept. He proved his abilities this night. He had become, with his performance at the Mandarin Hotel, the best trombone player in NYC. Joe and Charles backed him with the same verve and precision that they had ever backed Sam and Alice. They proved beyond any doubt their professionalism and their ability, but most of all that they were faithful, not only to their friends, but to the music itself. And with their help, Kidd had gone from a musician struggling to prove himself not only to himself and his audience, but to his friends up until that very last note was blown and the curtains once again fell upon the stage.

Kidd ended his set with the same uproarious applause that the entire group gathered after the opening performance. We all welcomed him behind the curtain and the nerves of this group of performers were starting to settle and the mood was turning once again to celebration. Keisha and I made ourselves comfortable backstage, readying ourselves for a long night.

Powell was the next on stage. He took no backup. Eiden pushed the piano centerstage and there Powell sat when the curtains parted. His intensity and concentration were unparalleled. He was easily the oldest performer in our gathering. Kidd being the youngest. Powell had been an NYC Jazz titan for two decades. He was beyond seasoned and still not past his prime. His passion played out through his piano with rapture, but his face and posture showed no such emotion. His exhibition was volcanic and contained, focused. A torrent of melody filled the hall and inspired his audience to dance. When he left the piano and the curtain's shadow cast down upon the stage, he walked back to the rest of us with just the slightest grin on his face.

Sam and Charles and Joe went on next. They had an understanding, a plan between them and they were in a state of bliss as the curtains parted and the stage opened. Sam blew a flurry of notes to start their set and Joe and Charles came in behind them. They swung a hot beat and the crowd responded in kind with dance and applause, unable to look on in still silence. Sam stepped aside and Joe stilled his sticks; Charles tapped out a solo rhythm that clucked his head, jerked his shoulders and tapped the toes of the audience. Joe rocketed in with a pure madness following Charles' solo and when he finished, Sam let a staggered moment of silence pass between the instruments before he blew out a cool bluesy stream of notes that ushered Alice on stage. And when she walked to the edge of that stage and parted her lips, she cast the same spell that had made her famous in the Jazz circles around town. She dazzled them, calmed them, and elated their audience with her delicate nature.

Their set, set the stage for Keisha. Erman set a stool for her to lean on. She plugged in her Fender. Her fingers glided through the notes and along the neck of her instrument as if they were intelligent life forms separate from her, independent creatures dancing on those metal strings. And then she sang with her throaty voice. She was slow and methodic. She soothed and quieted the rustling adulation of the crowd. She sang of heartbreak and romance, more heart aching Blues than feverish Jazz ... beautiful. Her voice pulled at my own heart as if she could pull it out through my chest and I felt sorrow, admiration, and love. It was a painful pleasure that she thrust upon her audience. It was a tender wrath that she projected through her voice, from her heart, and she ached and pained ten times more than anyone absorbing her song. She had deep, dark caverns within her that burned and spurned and tore at her and all she could do to quell her sharp fire was to spin and weave a song. As painful and difficult as it was for her to perform, as fragile and unarmored as it left her, it was her liberation to free her heart from those terrible bonds through her songs. She came to me when the curtains drew across the stage. Her skin was hot and her breath was slow and deep. She hung her arms over my shoulders and wept hot tears. Her cheek pressed against mine, wet my own face against hers, every aching cavern within her emptied during her song and I filled those newly empty spots with my silent longing. I pressed her against me and held her limp body in my arms. She was so delicate in this moment that I felt a fear creep into my heart; I was afraid that hurting her was inescapable, that healing her was impossible, that comforting her was the only salvation for my own heart.

Jarvis took the stage and Keisha and I started to settle into a calmer space behind the commotion of the stage and the audience. Jammin' Jarvis Wrightly is something else, someone unpredictable. He surprised me that night. I assumed that when he assumed the stage, it would be just him out there proving his talent, but not so. He certainly took center stage. He made a presence that was clear that he was the main attraction of his set, but he did not go on stage alone. He brought Joe and Charles with him. He brought Kidd with him. He even talked Powell into playing backup for him. Jarvis was not just a presence, he was a musical general and he proved his command along with his genius that night. I don't think it was a sign of magnanimity, his choosing to have so many of his friends and colleagues go on with him. It was a show of his superiority, but that was not exactly the feeling I got. The feeling that struck me was that in this show of unity he was also expressing that his presence was compounded and amplified by the talents of his friends. He blew his trumpet during his set with mastery and chose this night to show his experimental nature as well. He led his troop into hot beat and they swung and all up on that

232

stage, all involved showed their best side and they all played together. Keisha and Alice, Sam and I sat back. I could feel a cold chill of neglect between them, not being invited on stage with Jarvis. Though it was also a kind of compliment from him, that he didn't want to share his moment with them because he didn't want to be outshined. He didn't want to be outshined. Or maybe he wanted to give them a chance to relax and be entertained, which we were. And maybe still, he knew that there was no room for a song in his performance and left Sam out so that Alice wouldn't be left alone without him. Any which way it was meant, I think that everyone enjoyed Jarvis Wrightly's set; I know the audience did. They cheered for fifteen minutes with a solid wall of crashing applause before the final set of all the musicians, singers included.

Alice and Keisha talked before the final set. They were going to lead. They picked a song, an old Sarah Vaughn rendition of, It Never Entered My Mind. Suley once again walked on stage. He knew it was the final set, the hour was late and his monumental event had become a great success. All that was left was to close out the night with the same smooth precision that was incarnated by the first set and that flowed through everyone's performance as if this night were being watched over by seraphim.

Backstage, Erman was all praise and congratulations for the musicians. His words were a battle cry for the final fight. This small group of musicians, special forces is a good comparison, were stacked against a huge army in audience. It was their job to go out on that stage and slay that army, bring them to their knees and leave them with an experience they would be talking about for years to come.

Suley's final word to the audience opened the stage to the final show of the night. Alice and Keisha stood nearest the edge of the stage. Before they started to sing, the instrumentals pulsed out a tune that set the environment that opened a path for the throaty tones of Keisha's voice and the high melody of Alice's. Together, they were transient angels lifted by their band, carrying their audience to the heavens. The crowd was slain and delivered to their maker and the band went on. Keisha even played a solo on her Fender. Sam jammed out the sax, Jarvis the trumpet, Joe the drums, Charles the bass, Kidd the trombone, Powell the piano, and in the end was a pandemonium that spawned a cacophony that burst into a silence that ended the evening well into the ambrosial hours of the morning.

The final curtain fell; applause roused a victorious spirit among the crowd. Erman stood to deliver his final speech for the musicians. His smile was huge and toothy. His posture was that of a leader. He was proud and extroverted and spoke as a victorious general to his troops. We were all smiling as far as I knew and then out of what seemed to me to be nowhere; what was to me unexpected, Jarvis rushed Erman. I thought I saw the glint of a shining object in his hand. I couldn't make out what it was and didn't realize its significance until the stain at Erman's side grew. Jarvis stabbed Erman in the side and laid him gently on the stage and turned to us with a strange smile on his face. It was a coupe. It was insane. Erman was laying there on the ground bleeding and Jarvis, his assailant didn't even say anything; he just stood there staring at us as if he were daring us to object to his action. Well, I object, I thought and I moved into action. I rushed to Erman's side. How could I not. I brushed passed the lunatic. I fell next to my friend on the floor. I pulled out my phone and dialed emergency. I asked for an ambulance. I said my friend had been stabbed. Jarvis didn't touch me. He was pinned down by Sam and Charles. Joe stood over and stared down at Jarvis. Erman's eyes were all bewilderment. It's ok, man, I said. You're gonna be alright. I held his head in my hands. The knife was still in his side. I didn't know what else I could do. I just looked down at him and made sure his eyes stayed open, that he didn't pass out. That's all I gathered from TV and the movies. That's the only thing I knew about the situation, that it was important that he not pass out. He stabbed me, he said and his mouth was full of spit. He fucking stabbed me, he said. And he kept saying it over and over again. He fucking stabbed me!

Suley didn't know what was going on until the ambulance came. Somebody lead the EMTs back to us. Suley was rightly appalled and he rode in the ambulance with his old friend. Keisha and I took a cab to the hospital. Sam and Alice, Charles and Joe, Kidd, all the musicians that played that night, we all met in the emergency room. We sat together and waited to hear that he was alright. We were quiet; we were shocked; and I think we all felt a little ashamed about the way the night ended. Jarvis wasn't there. Jarvis was in a holding cell somewhere, waiting to learn whether or not Erman would press charges; he was left to learn if Erman would live or die and so his sentencing might change. Those of us waiting in that hopeless emergency room just waited for the words of good news. There was no room for the thought of death, not a night otherwise so joyous. No one could bring themselves to vocalize the question we all must have been thinking: why did Jarvis stab Erman? No one asked because we wouldn't get an answer. There was no real answer. None that would make any real sense anyway, not to anyone other than, perhaps, Jarvis. But I don't think any of us were interested in what he had to say.

Suley emerged with the doctor into the waiting area. We all stood up silently attentive to hear what we all hoped would be good news. Erman was certainly in critical condition, but his vitals had stabilized. The doctor was confident that after a few days of intense care, Erman would be well enough to leave the hospital and after six weeks, he would start to feel like himself again. We weren't allowed to visit him. But after hours of sitting around in that waiting room and after the intense show that everybody put on, we were all pretty limp and I for one had a nasty headache that I was eager to sleep off.

We all left at about the same time, leaving Suley at the hospital. He was going to stay with Erman for at least the night. He was beside himself and he was not in a pretty mood. He thanked us all for staying. Keisha and I were the last to catch a cab. We nodded in and out of sleep in each others' arms until we reached my apartment. I was so happy to be home, eternally thankful for my pillow topped mattress, the satin sheets. I fell asleep with her breath in my nostrils, her cool skin against my continually warm body. Her hair touched both our faces.

Chapter 33

The next time we met, Keisha's parents were in town. She didn't speak of them often. They were living in New Jersey. They left Upstate New York a few years after Keisha did. They lived in the part of New Jersey near Philadelphia, where they had grown up, the children of farmers. I've been down to that part of Jersey before, not far from Delaware, a beautiful, lush part of New Jersey not often enough associated with the State.

When Keisha asked me to meet with her and her parents for dinner one evening, I automatically said yes, excited about the thought. It made me nervous to think of meeting them. I had never met the parents of a lover before; all of my other romances were safely tucked away at my college campus. My nerves shuttered and shook me as I made my way to the restaurant, a classy Indian place on the Upper West Side that I cannot recall the name of.

Keisha's mother was a yoga instructor; her father worked maintenance in the oil industry. I didn't know there were refineries in South Jersey and Upstate New York … shows what I know. She hadn't told me much about her parents before that night, but apparently, she had told them about me. It made me feel good that this woman that I loved cared enough to talk about me with her family, that she felt comfortable enough and happy enough with me for me to meet them. My nerves settled when I sat at the table and sipped a glass of water. I thought that I was doing a good job presenting my best self, the best traits in my personality. I shook hands with her father and her mother. Her father was large and strong. Her mother was small, but somehow the more domineering of the couple. They did not remind me of my own parents. They were a different kind of people entirely. And there was a tension at the table, but I thought that should be a fairly normal ingredient to such a meeting. In the end, I felt good about the night. The food was good and there were a few laughs. I did make the mistake of offering to pay for the meal. I guess I just didn't know what I was supposed to do in the situation and felt that I should at least offer. I did not insist. Maybe I should have insisted. I had chicken masala. It was lovely. That's Keisha's word, 'lovely'. She used it sparingly, but often enough to associate it exclusively with her. This is how she described me to her parents. Right in front of me too. It made me glow a little I think.

Chapter 34

Day in and day out and I'm making the usual deliveries; I started to develop a strategy and a thicker skin for dealing with the bored housewives, the junkies who want me to get high with them and be their junky friends, the horny transvestites, the queers who talk your ears off. I couldn't make friends or cross boundaries with these customers. I presented a steely front, a static persona. I was a robotic, pneumonic, bionic man sort of delivery person, stone faced ... a total affront. I dazzled them with Armani Exchange and stonewalled them with total composure. I was a mystery, unshakable, unfathomable, a specter man. I actually felt cool about my new persona.

When I heard that Erman was out of the hospital and back at the Lounge, I jumped on the Vespa and motored down to see him. I was in high spirits. I felt good about the job again, about my girl, about my friends; I could feel my energy rising and I was high and happy about my condition in this city and on this planet.

His face was pale when I saw him, but he was smiling. Erman, back at his rightful throne at the palace of Suleyman. Erman, back in action, ready for the next big party. Well, maybe not quite ready for the next big party. He showed me his scar, a nasty thing on his right side. They had to sew up my guts too, man, he said to me before he gulped down some pride. I'm going to fucking kill Jarvis Wrightly, he said. That motherfucker! His voice wavered and shook, but he kept a mean composure. I told him that I hoped he wasn't serious. He smiled at me and said: he fucking stabbed me in the guts; he almost killed me. I almost fucking died, man. And somewhere in his angry voice, he thanked me for being there that night, for being the first person at his side. Hey, man, I said; you already did the same thing for me, you and Suley. You gave me the job that saved my ass. I'm a fucking high rolling, balling mofo … you know. He smiled at me. He was sitting. I was standing. I whapped him in the arm and we were buds and we laughed and he forgot his anger.

Chapter 35

My heart overloaded the day their album came out. The name of the album was Manhattan Underground: A JAZZ BEAT. Suleyman had arranged for a group photo to be taken after the show, the night of the show, but when Jarvis stabbed Erman, that train derailed. Instead, a talented young graphic designer, Lauren Israel, tailored something for the cover. Suley sent her an early, rough, unedited copy of the recording before the mass production. She poured over it for a week before she even started to work. Her end product produced a cover for the CD that was unique to the genre.

She declined to come to the party held at The Turkish Lounge. I never found out why. I never got to meet her. But the cover she made, made all my musician friends smile from one ear to the other. Keisha was especially outspoken about the design of the cover and the title of the album. She sat with her legs across my lap and her arms yoked around my neck. She nestled her face in my shoulder and kissed my neck. She swooned in the air of that evening and she whispered in my ear that she loved me. I had become a part of all this part of her life that she had dreamed one night as a little girl, a dream that she followed ever since.

We played the album all night long. We drank and we danced. Jarvis did not show up for the festivity. No one dared mention his name. Erman was on his feet for most of the night. He danced with several girls. He laughed his terrifying laugh. He was back and happy and ready for fun, though there was something new in his eye, a certain knowledge that comes from personal tragedy. I didn't mention that either. I only noticed it.

The night tore on. None of the musicians played and they were happy to display their commitment to the night, to the album, to each other. I danced with Keisha and laughed with all my friends and I felt like I was real, like I was a part of something special and sacred and whole. And I felt cool and happy ... free. I felt like I was just where I was meant to be.

The little hairs all over my body raised and fell and that special, human sensation washed over me and I shuddered with joy for a moment. And afterward I was just a man in the midst of a party with his friends, all dressed in high fashion, Manhattan sheik. Around us were painters and poets and dancers and sculptors and designers and creators and buyers and sellers and men and women and all of them were here to honor and praise my friends who circled around me and made me feel that I was one of them. At my side was the girl that made my heart soar, who made my skin hot, and my eyes shine. I could touch her and hold her and kiss her and know she was real and that she loved me with all her heart and all of her blood and she didn't have to say a word. I could see it in her eyes. And it was real.

Chapter 36

It was a Friday at dusk; I met Noah at Croxley's for beer and hot wings. We sat at a table and he was thumbing through a local newspaper. It was a casual meeting. Noah was between jobs. Not that he didn't have a job at the moment. He had already worked eight hours at his day job. He had only a few hours before he had to be at his night job. Noah is the epitome of the hardworking middle class Joe. He rarely complains. He always finds time to hang with his buds. I doubt that I am the only one to sit back occasionally and wonder where he finds the energy.

I had started my own day at four in the morning and had made my last scheduled delivery moments before I walked into the bar. My hours were long and erratic, but I just scooted around town dropping off dope and I got paid. Noah had two roommates and his was the small room. When we got together, work was done and forgotten. Noah was talking about the next show that he was excited about. Tonight he was torn between seeing the Hold Steady in BK or Lucero in Jersey City. He was pretty sure that he'd go for the Hold Steady. He knew those guys personally and Brooklyn was easier to get to. Oh, and the Hold Steady are awesome! What about work; I asked him. I've got it worked out, he said. And that was all that he said.

We were into our third beer before Noah shut me up with a proclamation of, holy shit! Don't you know this guy, he said. He was pointing at a picture in the paper. Jarvis Wrightly, he said when I asked him who was in the paper. At first when he said it, I thought it was just a write up in the music section - or something to that effect, but that wasn't the news at all. Shot three times in the chest, Noah read aloud, execution style. He was found in an alley outside a Jazz club in Harlem. I immediately thought of what Erman had said when he first got out of the hospital. I thought of his crazy laugh and that mean look I saw in his eyes. Jarvis had stabbed Erman two months earlier at the Mandarin Hotel. Erman never pressed charges. Jarvis walked. He walked down a dark alley after a show one moist Spring night where Erman or someone he'd hired found him alone and probably high or drunk or both.

The paper said that Jarvis's wallet was in his hand and that he had not been robbed. He'd offered his killer his wallet, believing that he was being robbed. The paper said that he had about seventy dollars in the wallet, no credit cards. Murder. One of my friends was murdered. One of my friends was a murderer. There was no doubt in my mind. Erman. This was his revenge for taking a knife in the gut.

       I didn't say any of that out loud to Noah. I just kind of froze and didn't speak after I snatched that paper away from him and read the entire article myself. After I read it, I was stuck in speculation. The details of the happening couldn't be known to me, but I had a good idea and there was no doubt in my mind that it was Erman's revenge. Noah was saying something. He started off saying he was sorry to hear that my friend was dead. I had told Noah that Jarvis stabbed Erman. I told him a few weeks before. It took him a few minutes to recall that conversation. When he said, hey - isn't that the guy who stabbed your Turkish friend. And then he started speaking his own speculations that were not too far from my own. Surely, Noah never heard Erman speak the words that I'd heard, that he was going to kill Jarvis, but he knew that I worked for him and what I did as a job. He knew the Turks were 'shady' characters. When he spoke the words, do you think your Turkish friend that was stabbed … do you think he killed this musician, he asked. I told him to shut up and he looked at me with pain in his eyes. I told him I was sorry, but you can't say that again. Don't believe it, I told him. As far as we're concerned, it isn't true.

I folded the paper and took it with me to the bar with our two empty glasses. I placed the paper on the bar and ordered another round for Noah and myself. I brought our beers back to the table and sat across from Noah and smiled and started a new conversation about the new Hold Steady album. It was a subject he was glad to assume and rattled on about his musician friends. They were rock and roll; they were underground, New York City style, but the members themselves, though they lived in Brooklyn, were Minnesota boys, or somewhere around there in the Midwest. I like the Hold Steady; they're fun and consistent good drinking music, not grunge, not punk – they had that new alt. rock style that hadn't really been named yet. It followed the lead of the White Stripes and Modest Mouse, but they carved out their own path from that more well known stream of thought and sound. Noah and I placed them in the same genre of rock as another upstart band that we were fascinated with, Lucero. They were a Tennessee rock band, a little rockabilly, a little grungy – the perfect music for young, alcoholic and brokenhearted.

Soon the time came for Noah to leave and go to his next job. He was a little drunk, but it was a rock club gig and it was pretty common for he and his coworkers to be a little drunk some nights. Neither of us were falling down. I was good enough to get back on the Vespa and I did. And as I rode away, I started thinking about Jarvis and about Erman. I didn't understand what that altercation at the Mandarin was all about. I couldn't figure out why Jarvis stabbed Erman or what was said just before he did. I thought about heading over to The Turkish Lounge and talking to Erman about it, but I'm no investigator and I didn't want to know, not really; I just harbored a sneaking curiosity that was better left un-sated.

I started up the West Side highway when my phone started buzzing in my pocket. I didn't feel like answering it. I was on my way home and hoping for a peaceful evening. Instead I took the next exit off the highway, pulled over and pulled out my phone. I missed the call, but it was Suley and I called him back. He wanted to know if I was holding. I told him that I wasn't, but that I had some money for him that I planned to drop off in the morning. He said to stop by The Lounge. I had to make a few deliveries. I sighed. I didn't want to see them tonight, not after the news. I didn't want to look at Erman. I couldn't imagine what it's like to be stabbed. But I never wanted to kill anyone either and I don't think that I would kill a man that stabbed me at a party. Well, maybe I would. How could I know? I didn't know how he felt. I know I'd be scared that a man willing to stab me might want to finish the job. But he could have just put Jarvis away in jail. Then again, maybe he was scared that Jarvis would tell of Erman's own misdeeds, a prospect that would have put my own safety, freedom and livelihood in jeopardy. What an ugly mess. I decided that I would act like I never knew that Jarvis was shot dead in some dark alley in Harlem.

  I showed up at the club. It was Erman who greeted me. It's the usual way, but tonight I was hoping to deal with Suley. No such luck. Erman acted like nothing was bothering him, like he'd committed no crime. But then again, his lifestyle was technically criminal and this is always as he'd seemed. I gave him the money I had from the earlier deliveries and he loaded me up with dope to deliver. Three spots in three very different areas of Manhattan. He gave me more than enough to satisfy the orders made which only meant that he was expecting more orders to come in while I was out. It was looking to be the beginning of a long night.

The first of the three places I stopped was in Tribeca, near the Knitting Factory. It was a very posh neighborhood that was always complaining about the noise the club made. It was a huge loft apartment. Three very pretty girls were there. I'd never delivered to them before and I thought it was a shame that such beautiful young women that could have easily been models would waist their bodies and minds on this shit. But as I'd decided earlier, I didn't say a thing about it. One girl handed me some cash and I gave her the dope.

My next stop was on the Upper East Side, not far from Hunter College. It was an old man dressed in tweed. He looked like a professor. I almost asked him what subject he taught, but I decided against it. He lived in a modest, well furnished apartment with a large library that took up an entire wall in his apartment. He had a lot of books on Physics, and cook books.

My third stop was at a huge apartment in Harlem. Harlem, that newspaper article was haunting me, preoccupying my mind and I hoped that no one was enticed to gun me down. I was sure to stay clear of any dark alleys. I know that over the years Harlem has developed a harsh reputation, but the Harlem that I met was a colorful, vibrant place with beautiful architecture and colorful personalities and the few times I'd been there -with Sam and Alice and the bunch- were times that I'd thoroughly enjoyed. I hated to have it personally associated with murder. I started to really hate Jarvis for stabbing Erman. Things could have still been good and pure in my mind. But all the ugliness of the world around me was starting to unveil itself and a shadow crept into my conscience.

Before I made it to the apartment door in that Harlem high rise, my phone started buzzing again. Erman had two more stops for me to make after that and then he wanted me back at The Lounge to drop off the cash and most likely re-up on heroin. I could feel a sickness grow in my stomach. The true reality of what I was doing, what I was involved in was starting to really sink in. All this had been a game that I hadn't really understood the consequences of. I knew this shit was bad for people, but after that night I started paying attention to things like statistics of murders associated with drugs, statistics of mortalities in NYC alone associated with heroin. I started to feel a real self disgust emerge within and I was starting to truly and understandably fear my employers.

Chapter 37

When I saw Keisha again, I didn't mention what I knew about Jarvis and what I thought about Erman. I was still feeling a deep unease and I hadn't slept well in the days before this meeting. It wasn't my conscience or the fact that I was upset about Jarvis and Erman. It was just that business was busy and I was running around all over town day and night, finding sleep a few hours here and there, more in The Lounge than at home.

Keisha didn't seem at all herself either. She even pulled away from me once or twice as I tried to nestle up to her. We were at her place in Williamsburg. A small place, but one that was comfortable and she decorated it well. It had a smell to it that was unique to Keisha and it was warm and clean.

We sat together on her couch. The television was on. She seemed unsettled and it took me an hour of prying to get it out of her what the matter was. She didn't want to talk about it, but it was bothering her and there was nothing else to catch her attention. She finally came out with it. Her parents didn't have much good to say about me. There were tears in her eyes and I sighed and I strained to understand what it was they didn't like about me. She said that her mother didn't trust me and thought that I was manipulative. I couldn't help but take offense. I put my best foot forward, used my manners – I gave them no reason not to like me. Her father didn't say a word on the matter. He was a stoic sort of quiet confident man. I told her that I thought they were very nice and that was my impression of them and I didn't think that I should have given them a different impression of myself.

Somehow this situation erupted into an endless and un-quell-able argument. There was nothing I could do to calm her on the subject. She was flat out crying when I left. And I left beside myself. All this world that had two months ago been the best life I could have imagined was starting to unravel. It was all I could do to hold back the tears and when Erman called me to work, I told him that I was sick and spending the rest of the day in bed. I called Noah. I needed to talk to someone, to a friend that would sit and listen, to have a drink and try to figure it all out, but I couldn't get a hold of him. I went home and showered and put on some sleeping clothes and crawled into bed. The sun was still up, dangling at the horizon. I cracked open a book and read until I fell asleep.

Keisha woke me at my door in the dead of the night. She was still crying and I wondered if she'd been crying the whole time since I left her in Brooklyn. I opened the door and she threw her arms around me. I pulled her in the door and took her back to bed with me. She didn't know how to feel, but she wasn't ready to let me stay angry with her. I told her that I wasn't upset with her; I just didn't understand anything that was going on around me anymore. I told her about Jarvis and that I thought that Erman was responsible and I told her that my job was really starting to get to me and I hadn't had a good night sleep in a while. And I hated that a rift was forming between the two of us. She calmed me. She held me and that night we were together and her mother's opinion didn't matter for a few hours.

In the morning she left and she was going to visit with her folks in New Jersey. I kissed her goodbye and started to fret and worry about them turning her against me. What had looked like fate from the outset was starting to worry me. A seed was planted in her mind and she planted that same seed in my own head and growing in our thoughts was the darkness of doubt. I was hoping for strength, but I felt a weakness growing within me. I didn't tell them I was a drug dealer, but I was. I didn't tell them that I had dabbled recently in hard drugs and it was in that world that I met their daughter. I was later to find out that they didn't even want her in this town and had been trying to coerce her back home for quite some time. As they saw it, I was the final lynch pin to unhook before they would have their daughter back. I didn't want to let her go, not without a fight; and that was the worst strategy to take, to fight – but I didn't see any other option.

Chapter 38

I remember the day the same way that I
remember childhood nightmares. It was mid-
afternoon and I was dropping off at Jarek's
apartment. He was giving me a hard time for
refusing to shoot up with him. I told him that I
was trying not to make a habit of it. He called me
a hypocrite and I shrugged it off. He tipped me all
the same and it was up till then a carefree day.

Just outside of his apartment, I hopped on
my scooter and started down the road when I
heard the siren. I made a swift turn down a side
street and the cop car screeched around the corner
after me. I felt a push of adrenaline surge through
my veins and I was in flight mode. I wicked the
throttle and raced away from them as fast as I
could and put a little more space between us, but
they were relentless and it didn't look like I would
be able to escape them entirely. The thousands of
thoughts in my head were screaming. It took a
moment and some close calls with some
pedestrians; I almost hit a couple of people, but

narrowly escaped that terrifying fate. I feared an accident that would compound the pains of any prosecution. For as much cash and heroin as I had on my person, I was facing a serious sentence. I could not get caught.

I raced East. I was already in the Lower East Side and the East River was my only hope of salvation. I tore across the FDR and dropped the scooter close to the wharf and reached into my pockets, pulled out the drugs and launched them as far into that wide river as they would go. I ran back to my scooter and the cops were running toward me. I was just about to hit the throttle when an officer easily twice my size caught my jaw with his fist and sent me flying toward the concrete. He picked me up and slammed me back down again; for good measure, I guess. He flipped me over on my stomach and fastened my wrists tightly with cuffs. I vaguely remember hearing him read me my Miranda rights.

He and his partner tossed me in the back of their car where I promptly passed out. They woke me harshly when we got to the station and they threw me in a holding cell. They didn't fish the evidence out of the river, thank God, but they threw the book at me for traffic violations: evasion, reckless endangerment, running several red lights, driving without a license, driving without insurance. It totaled over three thousand dollars in fines. All of which I plead guilty to on the spot and paid in cash. But before I left they gave me a good talking to. The arresting officer, Officer Grey, slammed me painfully against a cell wall and lifted me several inches off the floor by the collar of my Gucci shirt. He called me a bastard, an asshole, a low-life motherfucker. He told me he knew what I was up to and who I was working for. He told me I was in deep shit, that I was in over my head and if I didn't stop what I was doing, I would most likely spend the rest of my life in jail getting gang raped by murders. I knew he was trying to scare me; it was apparently a talent he had and he scared the shit out of me.

I paid my fines in cash and walked out the front door after spending five hours in the holding cell. They told me that the Vespa had been impounded in Brooklyn and gave me the address. My shirt collar was stained with my own blood. My mouth had been bleeding. I was shaking with fear and anger. This was it. I had to quit. I had to quit that day and I didn't want to go anywhere

near The Turkish Lounge for fear of being
followed.

It was a long, expensive ride into Brooklyn.
When I got the scooter back it had two flat tires
and all the lights and mirrors were broken. I
should have just left at in the impound, but I
wasn't thinking straight. I paid to have a mechanic
across the street replace the tires and the lights. I
called Suleyman and told him what happened and
that I couldn't work for him anymore and that I'd
tossed his drugs in the river and spent his money
on bail and impound and towing fees as well as
replacing the tires and lights. It was a loss of a day
and it was a long ride home from Far Rockaway.
With traffic and distance combined, it was well
into the night by the time I got home.

The first thing I did when I got there was to
pull out my stash of cash in a small box under my
bed. I sat on the floor and counted out every
dollar. It was well over eighty thousand dollars in
cash and I took a deep breath and let it back out
again. I sat there in a pile of money on my floor
and stared at nothing and breathed and sweated
and just sat there like a lump. I couldn't catch a
single thought for a while and time streaked by

like a subway that left the station just as I was arriving.

At some point I stood up and walked into the bathroom and vomited in the toilet and took a long, cleansing shower. I laid down in bed just as the sun started to break into my bedroom window. I slept without dreaming and when I awoke, I soon realized that two days had gone by. Thirty-seven hours straight by my calculation; it was a comatose slumber and when I woke, I felt dead. I felt lifeless. Only my eyes moved and they moved with little motivation. It had been a few weeks since I'd gotten a descent night's sleep. When I woke my jaw was sore and tight. When I woke I started to remember all the recent misfortune. And I felt a terrible pang of hunger in my stomach and total bodily weakness.

I walked into the kitchen and opened the fridge. There was nothing to eat. The eggs and the milk had gone bad. The mangos had shriveled and grown mold. There was a bottle of beer in the crisper, but I couldn't stand the thought of introducing alcohol to my empty stomach. I filled a glass with tap water and chugged it. I was so thirsty, my mouth felt like a wasteland.

I called up a nearby Chinese food restaurant and ordered enough food for three people and ten bottles of water. It felt like an eternity had gone by before the food showed up, but when it did, I snatched it from the delivery guy and didn't ask for any change, leaving the guy with over one hundred percent tip. It seemed appropriate considering how I made my money.

I sat on a couch in my living room and turned on daytime TV and vaguely watched as I shoveled dumplings and rice into my mouth, as I shoveled chicken and duck into my mouth, as I gulped down a bottle of water in one extended chug and shoveled and shoveled the food into my mouth. And when I could eat no more, I laid back on the couch with the pain of over-eating in my stomach and I fell asleep there in a mess of opened food containers.

I woke up in the middle of the night. I picked up one of the containers and started eating again. I was hungry again, but not nearly as hungry as I had been. I finished off the pork fried rice and the dumplings. I put the other containers in the fridge and threw out the empties. I walked into the bathroom and flicked on the light. I took a good look at myself in the mirror. I brushed my teeth. I washed my face. I shaved the thick and itchy stubble off until I was smooth faced again, bald faced again.

I camped out in my apartment for a few more days. I turned off my phone and put it in a drawer in my desk. I kept erratic hours. I watched tv. I read books. I watched movies. I masturbated. I wrote some bad poetry. I was, without a shred of doubt, freaking the fuck out. I couldn't even fathom the next step in my life, the next transition or possible solution.

Almost an entire week had passed before I snapped back into a cohesive state of mind. By that time I was ready to take out the trash, a ton of empty Chinese food containers, pizza boxes and assorted sized and shaped styrofoam food containers along with dozens of water bottles, soda bottles … beer bottles. I filled two large trash bags and dragged them out onto the sidewalk in my boxer shorts, a sweatshirt, slippers and my beloved Steelers ball-cap.

I took a shower and dressed like a Wall Street tycoon and took my phone out of the drawer and turned it on. I had several messages, none of which I was ready to listen to. I had ignored them every time I ordered in and immediately shut the phone back off and put it in the drawer. I called the limo service and had them take me to a little café on the Upper West Side. I ate a nice brunch and drank champagne. I felt like I was losing my mind. I left the café and started walking South. I walked and I walked until I got to the end of the island. I stopped there and looked into the water. I looked over the water to the statue of liberty. I smiled faintly and turned around. I started walking North until I got to Union Square. I stopped there and sat on the curved stairs before the statue of Washington. I sat and stared at the passersby. I sat there for at least an hour before I caught a cab home.

When I got back to my apartment, I disrobed and left my clothes in a pile on the floor. I was ready to listen to my messages. Sam called. Suley called. Mom called. Grandma called. Keisha called. I listened to each message and deleted each one after I listened to it. It was about ten o'clock. Too late to call Mom and Dad. Gram was probably still up, but I didn't call her either. I tried to make myself call Sam, but I couldn't get myself to do it. I didn't think it was a good idea to call Suley. I called Keisha. She'd left that message five days before. She was upset with me. She needed to talk. She asked if she could come over later. Sure, I said, but I didn't mean it. If she *needed* to talk, it couldn't be good.

She got to my place at around three in the morning. She was sober and tired. She apologized about coming over so late. She just got done performing. She rested her guitar in a corner of my apartment. I told her what happened with the cops. I told her that I quit my job. She said she understood. She said it was ok. She said she was glad that I quit my job. She stayed the night and we didn't have a serious discussion about anything. It was good to have her there. She brought me out of my head a little bit.

Chapter 39

In the months that followed my weird
reclusive/self-destructive spell, I tried to convince
myself that I felt normal, that I wasn't inhabiting a
turbulent inner space. I did this by attending a lot
of my friends' performances; I went to rock shows
with Noah. I ignored the fact that Keisha was
slipping away from me, that she was less and less
excited to see me, that she was spending more time
at her parent's home in New Jersey, that she took
longer and longer to return my phone calls.

I avoided The Turkish Lounge like the
plague, convinced that the cops were lurking in
secret shadows at every and any street corner. I
stayed out late and slept in, well into noon,
regularly. I dabbled with my writing but I was
struggling to grasp any tangible story.

One night, Keisha and I were out watching
Sam and Alice and Charles and Joe play at a well
established Jazz club in the West Village. She and
I didn't have much to say to each other. We didn't
touch, barely spoke. I was surprised that she

agreed to come out with me. She didn't dress up nice or anything, but then again, I hadn't bought her anything since I stopped working for the Turks. Sure I had a pile of money saved up, but I didn't have anything coming in. This is an expensive city and I couldn't maintain the lifestyle I did during the majority of our acquaintance, though it would be a shallow insight of mine to give the impression that our emotional separation had very much to do with money. She was having problems with dealing with her rising fame. She was overwhelmed by her parents' persistence and she was turned off by my increasingly nihilistic attitude. We were in for a good couple of nasty, private arguments. They were just around the bend and I could feel them coming.

　　Kidd played a set following Sam's usual group. He didn't sit at the bar with Keisha and I, when Sam and Alice and Charles and Joe were playing. I didn't know where he was at the time, but during his performance it became obvious that he had spent that time shooting up in the bathroom. I knew this because when he got on stage he looked like a sick zombie. He played like shit and when some unknown member of the audience called out to state that very sentiment, he stormed off the stage and didn't make it much farther than that before he started vomiting. He turned and fell back toward the stage and cracked his head open on the side of the stage. His blood and vomit mixed on the floor. The house lights went up and I saw the manager call for an ambulance. The crowd of onlookers: about half the crowd stayed and gawked while the other half left the club in revulsion. Keisha and Sam rushed to his side as he convulsed on the floor. He was overdosing and I just sat calmly at the bar sipping my beer. All I could think at the time was: I wonder if he's going to die. I didn't much care if he did or if he didn't. I was sick to death of junkies and drama and trauma and revenge and self pity and self destruction.

Kidd died on the floor of whatever that popular Jazz club was called. He died some small time before the medics rushed in the door with a gurney. I couldn't bring myself to care. I grabbed Keisha's arm and dragged her outside. I was drunk and surly. She was vocally upset with me. I tried to pull her in a cab and take her home. She resisted and resisted and we had a short screaming fight out on the street. I can barely remember the content of the argument that continued in the cab for about two blocks before she told me to go and fuck myself and got out of the cab.

It wasn't the last time I saw her. It wasn't the last time I spoke to her, but it might as well have been. I called her the next night and she wouldn't answer her phone. I left her a dozen messages apologizing for my previous night's behavior. I begged and pleaded and cried. She called me back a few hours later. We spoke softly to each other and she said she forgave me. I asked her over but she wouldn't come. I asked if I could go to her place, but she wouldn't invite me.

A week later we spent a day at the MET where I tried desperately to make small talk and find our once sparkling threads of passion for each other. But her hands were cold and I didn't have enough heat left in mine to warm her. She came back to my place anyway. I don't know why. I tried to seduce her. I tried to arouse her. I tried to find some way to reignite the passion that we'd had just a few months before. But it wasn't there. She allowed me to try to seduce her and arouse her but it was mutually frustrating and I made some terrible word choices to express my feelings on the subject. She dished out harsh words in response.

She left that night and it was the last time she set foot in my apartment.

She let me go over to her apartment a few days later, but that scene wasn't any better. She told me a few things that I cannot repeat and my response to her words were about as stupid and terrible as anything I'd ever said in my life. She could barely comprehend that she'd ever found me remotely attractive. We screamed at each other and she cried and I pulled out my hair.

In the weeks that followed this event were a series of awkward and confused conversations that only worked to place more tension between us. The last time I saw her or spoke to her was somewhere in the middle of Central Park. She called me out of the blue after a series of bullshit conversations. For some reason I had hope in my heart when I left to meet her. I tried desperately to make her laugh, but she only cried. She didn't say a word to me. She just looked at me and tears streamed down her face. She covered her face with the ends of her sleeves. She was wearing sweats, no makeup, no care went into her appearance. I was mutually frumpy and I only realize this in retrospect. We had become unimportant to each other and our emotions were splayed open by the memory of what we'd had. She would not let me hold her. She couldn't let me hold her hand and in the end, she wouldn't let me touch her or look at her face. Somehow I found a way to be shocked by all of this, as if I didn't see it coming.

This was it. The woman that I once thought would eventually become my wife and mother of my children. Her face was wet with tears. I could hear her sucking the loose mucus back up her nose. She wouldn't look at me or let me within a foot of her. I couldn't bring myself to cry. That came later. I just sat there. I couldn't leave her like this, but I wasn't allowed to console her. It was torture to watch her in such a display of sorrow and pain. At least I know that she did care and that it was hard and painful for her as well. But I love you, I said. I discarded my pride and those words only made her cry harder. I sat with her there on that park bench until she brought herself composure. She looked at me one last time and I searched her eyes for some glimmer of hope. It did not appear. She stood up. I stood up. I offered her a hug with open arms, hoping to feel her body against mine one last time, but she only turned and walked away. I watched her leave, hoping that she would return and wondering if she would even bother to look back. She did neither.

I turned to leave the park in the opposite direction. It started to rain. The rain started lightly, but quickly turned into a downpour. I couldn't bring myself to react to the rain by quickening my pace or looking for refuge. I simply started to cry. My tears started one drop at a time and then quickly turned to horrible streams that mixed seamlessly with rain coming down. My nose filled with mucus. My mind screamed in agony. My heart tore at me from inside. My world was over. Love was tearing itself out of my chest like an aborted fetus. I couldn't bring myself to leave the park. I got lost on its meandering trails. I prayed that the rain wouldn't stop. I didn't want any of the strangers to know I was crying.

I popped out of the park on the Upper East Side and hailed a cab. I sat as still and quiet as I could and tipped the driver well when he dropped outside my building. I opened the door and ran up the stairs to my apartment on the fourth floor. I fumbled with the keys before I got it in the hole. I opened the door and slammed it behind me and resumed crying. I fell to my knees and shook and shivered and wailed and lamented my terrible fate. I kept trying to figure out in my head where it went wrong, how I could have fixed it and how I still could. I kept thinking of plot lines and stories that insisted that true love always prevails, always triumphs over any and every obstacle, some worse than this, but the way she just cried and couldn't bring herself to even look at me. I felt hopeless and lost and broken and depraved and suicidal and tragic and stupid, fucking stupid.

Chapter 40

I couldn't bring myself to spend another week locked up in my apartment in a psychopathic depression. When I called Noah this time, he answered. I asked him to meet me at Croxley's for drinks. It wasn't a Friday and this request confused him. I can't, he said, I have to work. I asked him to take the night off to hang out. He didn't understand. I was in no place to spend the night alone or go out to a Jazz club and pretend that I was alright and I didn't want to go to The Turkish Lounge and numb my pain with drugs. I gave Noah the short version of what happened between Keisha and I; I told him she broke it off and I just wanted to get the hell out of my apartment and get shitfaced with a friend. He conceded. He said he'd meet me at Croxley's in two hours. He had to get someone to cover for him at work. He had to shower too. He'd only just woken up a little while before. He was sitting around playing videogames.

Noah was twenty minutes late showing up to Croxley's. I was working on three fingers of twelve year old Talisker with three cubes of ice. Noah came in and sat at the bar with me. He ordered a Smuttynose. He slapped me on the back and I smiled at him. Neither of us knew what to say so we just sat for a while in relative silence, sipping our drinks. You look good in jeans and a t-shirt, Noah told me. I laughed. Yeah, I said, I guess it's been a while since I haven't been trying to be something that I'm not. He laughed and stood up and alerted me of an open table on the other side of the room.

A waitress came over and asked if we were eating. It was about that time of day. Neither of us were hungry. I asked Noah if he wanted to switch to scotched. He laughed and said sure. I asked her to bring over the bottle, another glass and a cup of ice. I slipped her a C note and asked her not to bother us for a while. She smiled and said she'd check up on us about halfway through. I dropped three cubes of ice in each of our glasses and filled each half way up.

I asked him what he was up to these days, other than work. I asked him if he ever did anything other than work. I go out with you occasionally, don't I, he said. I laughed. It was nice to avoid the subject, though we both knew that we'd eventually get around to it. He was side stepping my question about the current events of his personal life which meant only one thing to me, that he'd met a girl and didn't want to bring it up and remind me of my recent loss. So, what's her name, I asked him. He smiled at me and sipped at the scotch. It's good scotch, he said. Damn right it is, I said. I persisted to know this girl's name. He said it was Beth. She was a little punkrock hottie. They met at a Hold Steady show. Kismet, I told him and scanned his face; he was genuinely happy. I told him that I thought that was great. He hadn't had a girl since I'd known him. I couldn't figure out how he found the time to even sleep let alone to form a romance.

The waitress came by and left us a fresh supply of ice cubes and asked if we were alright. We smiled and thanked her and she left us alone. Noah took hold of the conversation now that we had a good drunk on. He got the meat of our meeting. He asked a direct question about Keisha. What happened with you two, he asked – I thought everything was going good. Everything was good, I told him and then I didn't know what else to say, what all to disclose. It just got all fucked up, I told him and that was where I started to try to understand what happened for myself as well.

We stayed at that table a couple more hours and polished off that bottle of Talisker. Noah just sat there and listened and let me talk and try to figure out what the hell happened, how everything went from absolutely perfect to an absolute disaster. And in the midst of my slurred ramblings I called out in the middle of what was growing to become a very crowded bar that: she was the best lover I ever had. And I don't know if it was the memory of our amazing lovemaking or my embarrassment about exposing my private life in a crowded bar or the embarrassment that came from dishing out all this stupid insecure bullshit to Noah, but I could no longer hold back my tears. I covered my eyes with one hand as if it could do the trick that my eyelids couldn't.

I don't think that Noah knew what to do and I wished I could telepathically transport myself back to my apartment. I didn't have such powers. Noah called across the table in a loud voice, through the audible fog of the noisy room, Lucero is playing in Brooklyn – if we catch a cab

now we might make it in time to see most of the
show. It took a moment for his words to rattle
around in my clattering mind and make sense to
me. When his words sunk in, my tears stopped. I
wiped my cheeks dry and looked over at him. He
was forcing a smile and hoping that I would smile
back. I couldn't do that, not that. But I nodded at
him. Yeah, I said, let's go to BK. Noah was the
first to stand up. I stood up and had to grab hold
of the table to steady myself. The waitress caught
a glimpse of us and rushed over. We had to settle
our bill. I folded a couple crisp bills in her hand
and Noah and I made our way to the door, out
onto the street and into a yellow cab.

It started to rain as we crossed the Brooklyn
bridge. I leaned my head against the window.
The coolness of the window was good combat
against the heavy drunken feeling that was
overwhelming me. When we got to the club, the
rain had stopped. We got out of the cab and I
bummed a cigarette off some guy outside. Noah
stood with me and took a couple drags from the
smoke. There were a good couple people standing
around outside. I dropped the butt on the ground
and in we went. There was a small five dollar
cover which we paid. When we got inside, Lucero

was already on stage. The audience was young and hip. I walked up to the bar and bought a bottle of water. I chugged it down and bought another. I met back up with Noah in the crowd near the stage. Someone passed me a joint and I took a toke. It was a nice gathering; good people go to Lucero shows. Noah and I were quick to make friends for the night. We shared drinks and shared smoke and exchanged laughter and cheer. We even sung along to a few songs. In particular and my personal favorite ~ I was ecstatic when they played my all time favorite Lucero song, All Sewn Up. Just another heartbreak song, but in the mood that I was in that night, after what I'd gone through with Keisha, it was a healing prayer and an appropriate salve. The music that goes with the words are slow and Southern and the beat is one not quite of triumph as much as a self promise to keep moving on. And the words:

> All sewn up
> With bad tattoos
> All bit up
> Nothing to lose
> Well I've been a fool for oh so long
> Now the Mississippi mud cakes my boots

I'm afraid that I might drown if I don't move
From these waters that run so deep
From these Southern ways and lazy heat
Now I'm stuck
Ain't got much to show
With a little luck
Just watch me go
I've got torn up knees and calloused
fingertips
Broken vocal cords and busted lips
This goddamn guitar's never quite in tune
I'd leave it behind if it weren't all I could do
Now I'm stuck
Ain't got much to show
With a little luck
Just watch me go
Hell I'm all sewn up with bad tattoos
Can't hide from the faded truth
Well it follows me wherever I might move
All sewn up with bad tattoos
Well San Francisco sure sounds nice
And Brooklyn might suit me just fine
Well life down here just moves so slow it
seems
Like a river barge pushing upstream
Now I'm stuck
Ain't got much to show

With a little luck
Just watch me go
Now I'm all sewn up with bad tattoos
Can't hide from the faded truth
Well it follows me wherever I might move
I'm all sewn up with bad tattoos

It was my favorite song and it was the song to end their set and our night in Brooklyn. The gang of guys we'd been hanging out with were heading to an after party a few neighborhoods over and invited us to go. It was late. I walked with them for a few blocks before I found myself in the chair at a tattoo shop getting the image of a fool tattooed onto my shoulder.

Chapter 41

I woke up at five o'clock in the morning. I rolled out of bed and pumped out fifty pushups. I barely got those last ten pushups in. I laid face down on the floor and breathed and did twenty more pushups and laid face down on the floor and breathed. I did fifteen more pushups and laid face down on the floor and breathed. I did fifteen more pushups and laid face down on the floor and breathed. I pushed myself to my feet and showered. I shaved and brushed my teeth. I walked into my room and pulled on one of my wildly stylish suits, designer tie and shoes. I locked my door behind me. I took the stairs and walked out of my building. The sun was shining down on the streets, over the buildings. I sat on the Vespa and started her up. I revved its little engine and pulled out into the street.

I flicked through the turns and zipped down Broadway and across town into the Lower East Side. I pulled up in front of their building. I walked up the stairs. I knocked on the door.

There was no answer. I rang the bell. No answer. I peered in through a window. There was no blind or shade. There was no furniture or decorations inside. From what I could see, the place was empty. Empty? I wondered what was going on. I could have launched some kind of amateur investigation, but it seemed pointless. I could imagine plainly what happened. The authorities were obviously closing in. And with me, their buffer, gone and disappeared, all those customers, their illegal business grown out of a manageable proportion and they had made plenty of money here, especially once tallying in the best selling album they produced. The Turks had gone deeper underground. I wouldn't be able to find them if I tried. They didn't use modern technology. Their international connections were vast and powerful. They could still be in New York, or maybe they went to another State, or country. It's anybody's guess. I was only sorry that I wasn't able to give them a proper farewell. Though things ended in a frightening way, I will always remember the positive ways that our association effected my life. Goodbye my Turkish friends. I look forward to running into you again some day.

I descended their stairs, onto the sidewalk and sat on my scooter. I knew my next move. I rode over to the West Side of town to a road called the Avenues of Americas, in front of the headquarters of the New York Reader. I dismounted the scooter and walked into the building. The story that Suley had told me was fresh in my mind, of the mystery and excitement that had for the editor of the fiction department of this magazine been wholly enticing. The woman at the front desk tried to smoke screen me. I asked her politely to tell that editor that the writer George Wordworthy was there and would like to speak with him if he's not too busy. She asked me to take a seat and I did. I sat and I waited for some time and just as I was starting to get bored and fidgety, a tall, thin, well dressed man with grey, swept hair stood in front of me. I stood up and shook his hand.

We got to talking on our way to the elevator. He was happy to finally meet me and I was very happy to meet him. I thanked him for publishing my story. It was a great honor to have one of my stories in a magazine of the caliber of this magazine. When we got to his office, he offered me a bottle of water that I accepted. We got to talking about Suley. Then on to Audrey and Newspeak and the tragedy. I told him how I'd worked in the mailroom with Marc. He thought that was all very humorous and literary and he smiled and listened attentively. I told him that I found myself without a job. I told him that my experience began and ended with my work at Newspeak and that I wasn't asking for any large title. I just needed something to pay my modest rent while I started working on a novel of my experiences in New York City. He stroked his chin and looked at me with a smile. He must have thought I was some kind of a character. He took down my telephone number and jotted a short note next to it in his ledger. He said to expect a call from his assistant. He stood and shook my hand and walked me back to the elevator.

On my way out the door, I thanked the receptionist for her help and compliance. I was in high spirits. On my way home, I stopped off and picked up some Chinese food. I took it and sat at my computer and pulled up a word document. I turned on a Sarah Vaughn album and stared at the blank screen. I practiced my ability with chopsticks and popped pieces of General Tsao's Chicken into my mouth. The story was forming in

my mind and I thought I had a good idea of where
my story should start, with Grandma Trudy's
SUV, with Mrs. Nims and Columbia Presbyterian
Hospital. With an accident: 'If I close my eyes I
can still smell it. That smell of motor oil when it -
hits the hot outside of an engine...'

26910111R00164

Made in the USA
Charleston, SC
24 February 2014